Stripped Down

Also from Lorelei James

Rough Riders Series (in reading order)
LONG HARD RIDE
RODE HARD
COWGIRL UP AND RIDE
ROUGH, RAW AND READY
BRANDED AS TROUBLE
STRONG SILENT TYPE (novella)
SHOULDA BEEN A COWBOY
ALL JACKED UP
RAISING KANE
SLOW RIDE (free short story)
COWGIRLS DON'T CRY
CHASIN' EIGHT
COWBOY CASANOVA
KISSIN' TELL
GONE COUNTRY
SHORT RIDES (anthology)
REDNECK ROMEO
COWBOY TAKE ME AWAY
LONG TIME GONE (novella)

Blacktop Cowboys® Series (in reading order)
CORRALLED
SADDLED AND SPURRED
WRANGLED AND TANGLED
ONE NIGHT RODEO
TURN AND BURN
HILLBILLY ROCKSTAR
ROPED IN (novella)
WRAPPED AND STRAPPED (Nov 2015)

Mastered Series (in reading order)
BOUND
UNWOUND

SCHOOLED (digital only novella)
UNRAVELED
CAGED

Single Title Novels
RUNNING WITH THE DEVIL
DIRTY DEEDS

Single Title Novellas
LOST IN YOU (short novella)
WICKED GARDEN
MISTRESS CHRISTMAS (Wild West Boys)
MISS FIRECRACKER (Wild West Boys)
BALLROOM BLITZ (Two To Tango anthology)

Need You Series (debuts Jan 2016)
WHAT YOU NEED (Jan 5 2016)

Lorelei James also writes as mystery author Lori Armstrong

Stripped Down

A Blacktop Cowboys® Novella

By Lorelei James

[signed: Lorelei James]

1001 Dark Nights

EVIL EYE
CONCEPTS

Stripped Down
A Blacktop Cowboys® Novella
By Lorelei James

1001 Dark Nights
Copyright 2015 LJLA, LLC
ISBN: 978-1-940887-71-5

Foreword: Copyright 2014 M. J. Rose
Published by Evil Eye Concepts, Incorporated

All rights reserved. No part of this book may be reproduced, scanned, or distributed in any printed or electronic form without permission. Please do not participate in or encourage piracy of copyrighted materials in violation of the author's rights.

This is a work of fiction. Names, places, characters and incidents are the product of the author's imagination and are fictitious. Any resemblance to actual persons, living or dead, events or establishments is solely coincidental.

Acknowledgments from the Author

A 1001 thanks to the fabulous Liz Berry for all her love and patience with me—and for asking me to be a part of this amazing project.

And thanks to my readers who wanted to know more about Sutton Grant's brother Wynton, and London's pal, Mel. This love story is for you...

Sign up for the 1001 Dark Nights Newsletter
and be entered to win a Tiffany Key necklace.

There's a contest every month!

Go to www.1001DarkNights.com to subscribe.

As a bonus, all subscribers will receive a free
1001 Dark Nights story
The First Night
by Lexi Blake & M.J. Rose

One Thousand and One Dark Nights

Once upon a time, in the future…

I was a student fascinated with stories and learning. I studied philosophy, poetry, history, the occult, and the art and science of love and magic. I had a vast library at my father's home and collected thousands of volumes of fantastic tales.

I learned all about ancient races and bygone times. About myths and legends and dreams of all people through the millennium. And the more I read the stronger my imagination grew until I discovered that I was able to travel into the stories… to actually become part of them.

I wish I could say that I listened to my teacher and respected my gift, as I ought to have. If I had, I would not be telling you this tale now. But I was foolhardy and confused, showing off with bravery.

One afternoon, curious about the myth of the Arabian Nights, I traveled back to ancient Persia to see for myself if it was true that every day Shahryar (Persian: راىرهش, "king") married a new virgin, and then sent yesterday's wife to be beheaded. It was written and I had read, that by the time he met Scheherazade, the vizier's daughter, he'd killed one thousand women.

Something went wrong with my efforts. I arrived in the midst of the story and somehow exchanged places with Scheherazade – a phenomena that had never occurred before and that still to this day, I cannot explain.

Now I am trapped in that ancient past. I have taken on Scheherazade's life and the only way I can protect myself and stay alive is to do what she did to protect herself and stay alive.

Every night the King calls for me and listens as I spin tales. And when the evening ends and dawn breaks, I stop at a point that leaves him breathless and yearning for more. And so the King spares my life for one more day, so that he might hear the rest of my dark tale.

As soon as I finish a story... I begin a new one... like the one that you, dear reader, have before you now.

Chapter One

"Weddings make me horny."

Best man Wynton "Wyn" Grant turned to look at Melissa Lockhart, the curvy redheaded maid of honor. Today was the first time they'd met, so the comment threw him off—as had the other sexual remarks she'd made over the past two hours. Wyn wasn't sure if she was playing him...or if she wanted to play. He offered her a nonchalant, "Really?"

She smirked at him. "A strapping, handsome rancher such as yourself doesn't have anything to say to that besides...*Really?*"

Enough. He angled his head and put his mouth on the shell of her ear. "Gonna get yourself in trouble, you keep teasing me."

"You think I'm teasing?"

"Only one way to find out, ain't there?" He traced the rim of her ear with the tip of his tongue. "Words don't mean nothin' if you can't back it up with actions. And darlin' I *am* a man of action."

That caused a quick hitch in her breath.

He smiled and backed off.

After the last guests passed through the receiving line, Wyn's younger brother Sutton, aka the groom, snagged his attention. "The photographer wants a few shots of us alone, so can you—"

"Make sure the wedding party gets to the head table?" Wyn supplied. "No problem."

"Thanks."

Wyn's new sister-in-law, London, whispered something to Melissa.

Melissa leaned over, giving Wyn a peek of her magnificent tits. She attached the train to the back of London's wedding dress so it didn't drag on the ground. Then she straightened up and looked at Wyn.

He offered his arm. "The party waits."

She slipped her arm through his. "Such a gentleman."

Cres, Wyn's youngest brother, snorted. "Gentleman, my ass. He's been pullin' one over on you, Mel. My big brother is the biggest manwhore in three counties."

Little did his baby brother know that Wyn had been damn near a monk the past eight months, but he didn't bother to try and mask his playboy reputation. "Actually, I prefer the term man-slut," Wyn replied. "Manwhore implies that I take money for something I do very well. For free."

Melissa laughed. "You and I must be slutting around in different counties, Wynton Grant, because I don't have your name in my little black book of bad boys." She paused. "Yet."

They stared at one another with identical "bring it" challenges in their eyes.

And that's when he knew, without a doubt, his sexual dry spell was about to end.

"Oh for the love of God. You two have been eye-fucking each other all day. Just sneak into a horse stall and get it over with already," Stirling, London's sister, and the other bridesmaid, complained.

Cres's annoyed gaze flicked between the best man and the maid of honor. "Take Stirling's advice. And don't even think about givin' one another head beneath the head table. Tonight ain't about your uncontrollable urges." He paused. "Got it, Super Man-Slut and his new sidekick, Slut-Girl?"

Wyn struck a superhero pose and Melissa snickered.

After heaving a disgusted snort, Cres muttered to Stirling and they started the trek to the reception hall.

"I do believe I'm offended," Melissa drawled. "My sidekick name should've been *Amazing* Slut-Girl at the very least."

He laughed. "Come on, Melissa. Let's see what kinda dirty, dastardly deeds we can get away with."

"Deal. But call me Mel."

"Mel? Nope. Sorry. No can do."

"Why not?"

"Mel is the name of a line cook. Saying, 'Suck harder, Mel,' or 'Bend over, Mel,' brings totally different images to my mind than 'I'm gonna fuck you through the wall, Melissa.'"

"I see where you're coming from, cowboy." She paused outside the sliding wooden doors that led to the lodge. "But that just means I'll be calling you Wynton—even when you're not making me come so hard that I scream your name."

"Darlin', you can call me anything you like as long as I get to bang the hell outta you tonight."

"Oh, there will be banging. But I'm gonna make you work for it to see how bad you really want it." Her eyes danced with a devilish glint that tightened his balls.

"That ain't gonna scare me off." Wyn let his gaze move over her, taking in every feature. From her cinnamon-colored ringlet curls to the broad angles of her forehead and cheekbones. From her bee-stung lips to the pointed tip of her chin. Then down her neck, noting the smattering of freckles across her chest and the plump breasts. Moving down her torso, imagining softness and curves beneath the long, emerald green dress. He took his time on his visual return, mentally shoving her dress up to her hips, pinning her against the wall, feasting on her skin from neck to nipples as he drove into her over and over. Finally his eyes met hers. "I love a challenge."

Inside the lodge, it was obvious London's parents had gone all out for their oldest daughter's wedding. The ceremony itself had taken place in a meadow on the Gradsky's land. One of the few places—according to London—that wasn't a horse pasture. Even the weather, always iffy in October, had cooperated, filtering autumn sunshine across the meadow grasses, creating a dozen shades of gold against the backdrop of a clear, vivid blue sky. After the simple ceremony, the newlyweds had hopped into a horse-drawn carriage. The wedding guests were loaded onto flatbed trucks—a fancier, classier version of a hayride—and returned to the lodge for the receiving line and reception.

"Isn't this magical?" Melissa said with a sigh. "It fits London and Sutton so perfectly."

"That it does," he murmured. Strands of lights were hanging from the rough-hewn log rafters and twisted around the support poles. Centered on each table was a lantern bookended by mason jars filled with flowers in earth tones ranging from gold to russet. Shimmery white tablecloths were tied at the edges with coarse twine—a mix of elegant and rustic.

He glanced at the far corner of the enormous room and saw a band setting up behind a large dance floor. A makeshift bar had been erected in the opposite corner, coolers stacked on top of hay bales and bottles spread across a wooden plank. Long buffet tables stretched along the wall. Beneath those serving dishes was beef raised on the Grant family ranch. Wyn had checked out the slow-cooked prime rib prior to leaving for the ceremony. Between family, friends, and Sutton's rodeo buddies, as well as the

Gradsky's big guest list, he suspected there wouldn't be many leftovers.

"Whatcha thinking about so hard?" Melissa asked.

"Food. I'm starved."

"Me too. I hope the photographer doesn't keep the newlyweds forever. At least being in the bridal party, we get to eat first."

Cres and Stirling were standing in front of the head table with guests crowding around them.

"Looks like our receiving line duties ain't quite over yet."

Wyn steered Melissa to the other side of Cres so any well-wishers would have to talk to them first—even after the bride and groom slipped in.

It turned out that these few stragglers had skipped the receiving line and were looking for a private word with the newlyweds. Wyn kept his smile in place as he repeatedly told the guests that the bride and groom were finishing up with pictures. He had no patience with people who didn't listen to the announcements or thought they were above the rules.

"I hear you growling between guests," Melissa whispered.

"I don't like the unspoken sense of entitlement. Every one of these people should've just waited in the damn receiving line like everyone else."

"Agreed. I'm glad Sutton and London aren't being bombarded with this. They deserve a little time alone, away from the maddening crowd."

Melissa's smile tightened when the last couple approached them.

Breck Christianson whistled. "Mel, you're lookin' fine. Damn girl. I thought maybe you'd turned into one of those binge and purge kinda chicks at the beginning of the rodeo season. Skinny as a wild dog. Then here you are. Back to all those plump curves."

Wyn didn't bother to bank his annoyance with this blowhard. He'd never liked Sutton's rodeo buddy and he liked him even less after that bout of verbal diarrhea. "I don't know if you're already drunk or what, but sayin' that bullshit to her ain't gonna fly with me."

Breck's eyes narrowed. "Who the hell are you to tell me what I can and can't say to an old friend?"

"I'm a man who won't put up with your disrespect because from what I hear, you do this all the time. So it ain't happening at my brother's wedding."

"Jesus, Mel, are you dating this guy?" Breck asked.

"Doesn't matter," Wyn said coolly. "What does matter is telling Melissa you're sorry for bein' a loudmouth."

"Or what?" Breck challenged. "You gonna pound on me, tractor jockey? I throw down steers bigger than you every damn day."

"Breck," Cres said sharply. "You're bein' a jackass. Knock it off and move on."

Breck leveled Cres with a dark look, but Cres didn't back down. Then Breck dropped his arm over his date's shoulder. The miniature-sized bleached blonde barely reached the center of Breck's chest.

Her sneering gaze rolled over Melissa and Wyn from head to toe. "They're not worth your time, Brecky."

Melissa held in her reply until the obnoxious couple drifted away. "How the mighty have fallen. It looks like *Brecky* had to buy a bargain basement escort to the wedding. The idiot has lost a lot of friends in the past year." She stood on tiptoe. "Thank you for calling him out on his lack of tact." She brushed her mouth over his ear, sending a shiver down the left side of his body. "But you didn't have to do that to impress me, because Wynton, I am a sure thing tonight."

Wyn nudged her chin with his shoulder, forcing her to look at him. "I did it because he was outta line. Had nothin' to do with how crazy I am to taste the freckles on the back of your neck as I'm driving into you from behind."

Desire turned her light-brown eyes almost black. "Gonna be hot as a brushfire between us, Super Man-Slut."

"For right now we'll have to settle for a slow burn, Amazing Slut-Girl. Shall we take our seats?"

* * * *

The bride and groom finally made an appearance half an hour later.

Evidently Sutton was starving because he pushed back speeches, reception games, and dancing until after everyone had eaten.

Then Wyn was so busy shoving food in his mouth and seeing to his best man duties that he didn't have a chance to talk to Melissa privately until over an hour later.

He grabbed a beer and sat beside her. "Hey. Did you get enough to eat?"

"Too much. The food was great." She propped her elbow on the table and rested her chin on her hand. "When you disappeared for so long I thought maybe there was an emergency that only Super Man-Slut could handle."

"And not invite my trusty new sidekick, the Amazing Slut-Girl? Not likely." He sipped his beer. "Why? Did you miss me?"

"Yes. We had a very...promising conversation going and then the Injustice League split us up."

He laughed. "I don't know what the hell Cres's problem was." Wyn and Melissa had taken the two chairs on the other side of the groom's seat at the head table. But Cres and Stirling insisted the setup was groomsmen next to the groom and bridesmaids sat on the bride's side. So it *had* seemed like they were purposely being separated. "Anyway, great toast."

"Yours was good too."

"Glad it's over. I ain't much on public speaking." He set his forearms on the table. "And while you were talkin', I noticed you have a hint of a drawl. Where are you from? Texas?"

"As if. I'm from the great state of Kentucky."

"That didn't sound real sincere."

"I used to be all *Rah! Rah! Go Wildcats!* But I grew up, moved away, and haven't been back to the Bluegrass State for more than the occasional weekend since I graduated from college."

"A Kentucky college girl. So what's your degree in?"

"American literature with an emphasis on twentieth century authors."

"Huh." Had she noticed his eyes glaze over? "So uh, what do you do with that degree?"

"Exactly."

Wyn blinked.

"I would've liked to teach—I still would—but earning a degree was secondary to why I attended UK."

"And why's that?"

"I went to school there to be part of their equestrian team. Train with the best, win a team collegiate championship, compete individually, and qualify for world finals with the end goal of competing in the Olympics." She sipped her drink. "Bored yet?"

"Are you kiddin'? Lord, woman, you're a Kentucky blueblood from a horse training dynasty or something, aren't you?"

"I was, now I'm not. Now I..." She shook her head as if to clear it. "This year, I've been teaching at Grade A Farms. Chuck and Berlin Gradsky have...shall we say, affluent clientele who prefer their children train in the English style rather than western."

"Well, Kentucky, I'll bet your horse cost more than my house."

"But you own your house. I never owned my horse. My parents' corporation did. And when I was competing I leased my horse from Gradskys."

"You're not competing anymore?" He didn't remember what her rodeo specialty was. Since she'd gotten the horse from Gradskys, he'd put money on her being a barrel racer.

"How did I end up blathering on? It's your turn." Melissa stared at him expectantly.

Wyn shifted in his seat, feeling uncomfortable with her for the first time since they'd met.

"Don't." She squeezed his knee beneath the table. "This is why I don't tell people about where I came from. I'd rather they see me as a rodeo road dog who gives it the almighty try year after year but never *quite* makes it to that top tier."

"That's intentional, isn't it? Not competing on the highest level?"

"I had enough of that. Now I drift from town to town and occasionally toss out a Sylvia Plath quote or a passage from William Faulkner to keep people guessing about me." She squeezed his knee again. "You were about to spill all of your secrets to me, Mr. Grant."

"That's one thing I don't have are secrets. I grew up a rancher's kid and never wanted to do anything else. When it became obvious that Sutton was better than average with his rodeo skills, I knew he wouldn't want to ranch full time, so I stepped up and learned everything I could. Figured it'd be up to me'n Cres to keep the ranch goin'. My folks did insist on shipping me off to vocational school for three years."

"What's your degree in?"

"Associate degrees in engine repair and veterinary science." He sipped his beer and smirked at her. "Granted, it's no Elizabethan poetry degree, but it's helpful around the ranch knowin' how to doctor up machines and animals."

"Elizabethan poetry? Nice shot, grease monkey."

He laughed. Damn he loved her sense of humor. "You had that comin', Kentucky."

Her eyes turned serious. "Why is this so easy with you?"

"Because we're both easy?" he offered. "It's easier knowin' how things are gonna end between us tonight."

"You two look awful cozy over here," a cooing female voice broke the moment.

Wyn looked up at Violet McGinnis. Then he leaned back and draped his arm across the back of Melissa's chair. "Hey, Violet." After spending one night in Violet's bed, she decided they were destined for each other. Not because the sex was off the charts explosive. Not because she was crazy about him and wanted to spend the rest of her days with him. Her sudden interest happened after she'd turned thirty and decided to settle down. He'd never been interested in that with her, or any other woman, and hadn't hidden that fact from anyone. But she hadn't taken the hint.

Evidently it was time to broaden that hint.

"We are very cozy," Melissa said, pouring on a thick drawl. "In fact, we may not move from this spot all night, it's Super"—she caught herself and amended—"that me and my best man are hanging."

Violet crossed her arms over her chest. "I hope that's not true because Wyn promised me a dance."

"When did I promise you a dance?"

"It's a figure of speech, Wyn, meaning I want to dance with you."

"Ah. Well, I wouldn't want you turnin' down all the other fellas who're eager to squire you around the dance floor on the off chance I'll tear myself away from this lovely lady's side tonight. Because I doubt that's gonna happen."

Violet didn't know how to respond. She spun on her boot heel and stormed off.

"Recent conquest?" Melissa asked.

"Eight months ago or so."

"She lousy in bed?"

"Not that I recall."

"So why no repeat?"

Wyn watched Violet move to the back of the room. "That'd give her the false expectation there might be a three-peat. I'm not interested in settling down with her. Or anyone else."

"That's another thing we have in common. But there seems to be...a few haters, here, Super Man-Slut. So how many women in this place have you nailed and bailed?"

He scanned the tables. "Six?"

"You're not *sure* how many women have slicked up your pole, grease monkey?"

"Funny, Kentucky. You say that like you didn't admit, two short hours ago that you're equally as slutty as me."

"Fair point."

"Lots of people from the world of rodeo here. How many guys have you mounted and discounted, Amazing Slut-Girl?"

"Mounted and discounted." She snickered. "That's a new one. I might have to steal that." Melissa tried to discreetly crane her neck to scan the area. After several moments, she said, "Four. Five if I'm counting the same guy but two different times."

"Nope. Still only counts as four. But I *am* interested on what he did that earned him a second go."

"He was breathing."

Wyn choked on his beer. "What the hell?"

Melissa shrugged. "All right, it was more boinking from boredom. We ended up at the same after party. Other people started hooking up so we were like...you'll do. How close is your horse trailer?"

"Has he been eye-ballin' you?"

"Some. But I'm not interested in ballin' him, because that'd be a three-peat rule violation and like you, I don't raise false hopes." She cocked her head. "But I'd make an exception to that rule for you."

"You know what I like about you so far, Kentucky? You don't make excuses for bein' a highly sexual woman."

"And?"

"And you said you were gonna make me work for it. Since we're bein' open about everything else, explain how. Because I want a piece of you like you wouldn't believe." Wyn pushed to his feet. "I'll be right back."

Chapter Two

Mel, you are in deep with this man and you've known him less than half a day.

She watched Wynton Grant amble off. And she couldn't help but notice other women sizing up the rancher hottie too.

From the moment she'd set eyes on him she had that overwhelming punch of want—a feeling that happened to her so rarely lately. So seeing the identical look of lust sizzling in his eyes? The balls to the wall woman of action who'd been in hiding for the past six months had awakened with one thing on her mind.

Sex.

Lots of it.

Hot and dirty sex.

Fast sex.

Slow sex.

And it turned out the very sexy best man was more than happy to oblige.

This was turning out to be the best wedding ever.

The object of her lust stopped to speak to an older woman, giving Mel ample opportunity to study him. The man had it going on. His shoulders were so broad that he blocked the view of the woman entirely. Pity he hadn't taken off his western cut suit coat so she could check out his ass; she'd bet his buns were grade A prime beef too. Not only did he have a big physical presence, he carried himself with confidence. He had an easy smile—which was a sexy-as-his wicked grin. From the back she noticed his dark hair brushed his collar and held more than a little curl. The groom and groomsmen had removed their cowboy hats as soon as the wedding pictures were done. As much as she appreciated a man in a hat, Wynton looked better without it.

Hands landed on the back of Mel's chair and a soft rustle of fabric tickled her neck.

"Staring at him that intently won't make his clothes disappear," London murmured in her ear.

"That obvious?"

"Yes. But if it helps, my brother-in-law is staring back at you the same way."

"Then maybe I'll get lucky on your wedding night too, Mrs. Grant."

London plopped down in Wynton's chair. Her wedding dress was a stunning mix of ivory satin and chiffon. Intricate beadwork of rhinestones and pearls stretched across the bodice of the off-the-shoulder dress. Folds of satin were ruched below her breasts and then floaty, filmy panels of chiffon fell in a column to the floor. It was simple and elegant—exactly like London herself.

"So you'll get a kick out of this, but you cannot tell anyone." London leaned in close enough that a long tendril of her hair touched Mel's cheek. "Earlier, when Sutton said the photographer wanted pictures of just us? Total lie. My husband insisted we have some alone time. And by alone time I mean us in the ready room, with my wedding dress pushed up to my hips, Sutton's tux pants around his ankles as he proved how much he loved me by immediately consummating our marriage."

Mel grinned. "Sounds like him."

"He said he didn't want to wait hours to finally claim what was legally his forever."

"If I didn't love you so much I'd hate you. That's so freakin' romantic."

"I know. I'm so lucky. I am such a sucker for that man. He keeps trying to get me..." She sighed. "Look, I need you to do me a favor."

"Anything."

London tucked a key into Mel's cleavage. "Keep this away from me. And definitely keep it away from Sutton."

"What is it?"

"The key to the ready room where we already rocked the countertop. I have to tell him that I lost it because if he had his way we'd be in there right now. I understand this is a celebration for everyone else, so I can share him for a few more hours. But I promise we ain't gonna be here all night."

"Everyone will expect you to take off."

"Speaking of expectations...You've been such a huge help to me throughout the wedding planning. Mom and I couldn't have done it without you."

Mel teared up. "My pleasure. But if you would've turned into Bridezilla at any point, I would've bitch-slapped you."

"And that's why I love you." London hugged her. "But don't think for one second that I'm not aware there's been some serious shit going on with you the last six months. You can talk to me about anything. So I'm telling you that you *will* be spilling your guts to me as soon as I return from my honeymoon, got it?"

"Yes, bossy-pants."

"That's *Mrs.* Bossy-pants to you." London whispered, "Thank you for being my maid of honor, Mel. Thank you especially for being the sister of my heart."

The tears she tried to hold back fell freely. "Same goes."

"You have your own special chair, my darlin' sister-in-law, so get outta mine," Wynton said behind them, "and quit hoggin' my wedding partner."

"I'm goin', I'm goin'."

After he sat, he noticed Mel's damp cheeks and he looked at London sharply. "You made her cry?"

"They're happy tears, I promise," Mel said with a sniffle.

"So you weren't here warning her off me?" Wynton asked London.

"I should, because you're a serious pain in my ass. But I kinda like you, Wyn, so I'll take the high road and not fill her in on your many conquests." London winked. "His little black book rivals yours, Mel. So I'm thinking you two might be a match made in heaven."

He laughed after London flounced off. "Love that girl."

"Me too."

A voice boomed over the loudspeaker. "Let's kick off the festivities with the bride and groom's first dance as a married couple. Sutton and London, take the floor please."

Wynton scooted his chair closer. "Will you cry when you hear the song he chose?"

"Maybe. This part and the father/daughter dance always make me cry." Her eyes narrowed. "Wait. What do you mean the song *he* chose?"

"Sutton asked London if she trusted him to pick a first dance song and surprise her."

"So you know what it is?"

He nodded. "And trust me, Kentucky. You're gonna need more tissues."

Turned out, he was right.

* * * *

Ten minutes later, when she and Wynton were on the dance floor with Cres and Stirling, the newlyweds, and both sets of parents, Mel still had a lump in her throat thinking about the song Sutton had picked. Billy Joel's "She's Got A Way."

"You all right?" Wynton murmured.

"No. I'm just so happy that London found the perfect man for her. Sutton...gets her. I never would've pegged him as the romantic type."

"Yeah. Me neither. He told me she makes him a better man. I guess that's something to aim for in a relationship." Wynton smiled against her cheek. "I'm happy for him too." He paused. "Maybe a little jealous."

"Jealous? You? Mr. I'm-not-settling-down?"

"From a strictly competitive point of view," he explained. "I'm the oldest. I should've gotten married first."

Mel tilted her head back and stared into his eyes. "I call bullshit on that. Nut up and admit you want that." She pointed at the happy couple.

"Fine. I want that. Someday. How about you?"

"Of course I want it. When I'm lucky enough to find the one."

The DJ called for all the guests to join the wedding party on the dance floor. And although people crowded around them, it seemed as if they were the only ones in the room.

"What makes a man 'the one' Melissa?"

The husky way he rasped her name sent a slow curl of heat through her. "Not wanting anyone else. Everything you do, everything you are with that one person is enough."

"I never thought of it that way."

"It's logical. The literature degree allows me to break anything down to its most basic component. Even love."

"No, baby, that romantic notion of 'one true love' is all you, and logic won't play into it at all when you find him."

And...she melted. "I really want you to kiss me right now."

"I really want to take that pretty mouth you're offering, but not here." He brushed his lips across her ear. "Dance with me. Let's both of us take the time to enjoy the journey for a change. Since it sounds like we both jump to the good part first."

Mel was beginning to believe being in Wynton's arms *was* the good part.

The tempo changed to a fast tune and he eased them into a two-step. They danced four songs together. When it came time for the father/daughter dance, he draped his arm over her shoulder and wordlessly pulled a tissue out of his pocket when she started to sniffle.

He excused himself to dance with his mother, and Cres whisked her back onto the dance floor when he saw Breck approaching her. After that, Mel danced with London's dad, London's brother, Macon, the wild bulldogger Saxton Green, and Sutton's boss.

By the time she returned to the head table for a drink, she realized the dizzy feeling wasn't just from dancing and she needed a quick snack to keep her blood sugar in check. She cut to the bar and downed a glass of orange juice. She turned around and Wynton was right there.

"I saw you slam that."

"I was thirsty."

"So it appears." He drained the contents of his lowball glass and set it on the tray. "I like dancing with you, Kentucky. Come on." He clasped her hand in his and led her to the dance floor.

She nestled her face against his chest and murmured, "I like dancing with you too, cowboy."

At the start of the second slow song, Wynton said, "Most dangerous place you've had sex, Amazing Slut-Girl."

If it was anyone else, she'd be surprised by the question. "Against the pen that housed the bulls after a rodeo. I kept waiting to get rammed in the back by a horn. It didn't last long, if I recall. How about you, Super Man-Slut?"

"In my high school girlfriend's parent's bed. We'd just finished when we heard the front door open. We had no choice but to dive into the closet. But her parents were in the mood and they ended up goin' at it on the floor—on the other side of the bed so we didn't get a floor show, thank God. But my girlfriend was horrified. She was even more horrified when her dad said if he caught us doin' it, he'd cut off my cock and send her to a convent. We broke up the next day."

Mel laughed. "The one time I remember getting caught I almost bit off the guy's dick. He assured me that he and his girlfriend had called it quits. I'm in his camper, giving him a blowjob, and the 'ex' girlfriend walks through the door—turned out they weren't broken up. She's pissed, I'm pissed, the dude is about to piss himself, so of course he suggests he's willing to share himself and maybe we both oughta blow him at the same time and then do each other."

"While he watched."

"Of course."

"Jesus. Some men are idiots. What happened?"

"I apologized to her and she broke up with him on the spot. We went to the bar, ended up doing blowjob shots all night and became fast friends."

"I call bullshit on that." Wynton tipped her head back and gazed into her eyes. "Aw, hell. That's how you met London, isn't it?"

She smirked. "I'll never tell."

"So have you been in a threesome?"

"Yes. More than one. You?"

Wynton smirked back. "Yes. More than one."

"Well, shoot. We *are* evenly matched in slutting around." Mel decided it was time to kick up the competition. "Ever fucked a famous person?"

"Define famous."

"If you said the name I'd know it."

He shook his head. "How about you?"

"Yes, I have. But I will qualify that by saying he wasn't famous when we fucked, and it lasted like thirty seconds."

"Who was it?"

"Sorry, cowboy, I don't kiss and tell details. But I have no problem giving a general overview of my sexual exploits."

"Same. But to be honest, I don't have anyone in my life who wants to hear about the kinky things I did. So I've stored up all my happy endings—"

"In an impressive spank bank?"

A beat passed, then Wynton threw back his head and laughed.

That single, spontaneous expression of joy moved her. Given their raunchy subject matter, she expected he'd toss out a few lewd vibrator references, but his laugh seemed a more genuine response than trying to one-up her.

"What's so damn funny over here?" Sutton asked.

Mel and Wynton had been so deep in conversation they hadn't noticed the bride and groom dancing right next to them. With very curious expressions on their faces.

"We're just swapping bad sex stories," Wynton said without hesitation. "Why? Did you need us to do something official?"

"Shots of tequila!" London said, pumping her arm in the air.

Sutton grabbed her arm and returned it to his neck. "Behave, wifey-mine, or I'll have to take you over my knee."

"Were you two talking about bondage games?" London asked. "Because while I appreciate my husband's rope expertise, I think turnabout is fair play, don't you? Shouldn't I get to tie him up sometimes?"

The groom blushed and whispered in London's ear. Whatever he said made her eyes glaze over and put a cat-like curl on her lips.

Mel glanced up at Wynton, expecting to see amusement in his eyes, but the longing she saw made her ache. He wanted that same connection his brother had more than he wanted to admit.

Don't you too?

"We came over to remind you that the bouquet toss and garter removal is happening soon," Sutton said. "We'll stick around for maybe an hour and then we're takin' off."

"We're at your command," Wynton deadpanned. "But there's something I've got to do first." He kept ahold of Mel's hand as they exited the dance floor.

She had no idea what was going on. When it appeared they were headed to the bar, she started crafting excuses on why she couldn't do shots with him. But Wynton strolled right past the bar and out a rear exit.

It had gotten chilly since the sun had set. Mel shivered, wishing she'd grabbed her wrap.

Then she found herself absolutely burning up, pressed against the side of the building by two-hundred pounds of hot cowboy. Good Lord. The heat in Wynton's eyes nearly set her skin on fire.

There was no speech about how much he wanted to kiss her. He just did it. Lowered his head and planted his mouth on hers.

He didn't have to prove he was a passionate man by thrusting his tongue past her lips and into her throat. He proved it with tender nibbles and teasing licks. A gentle pass of his mouth. Again and again. As if he had all the time in the world.

Each time Mel parted her lips ever so slightly, breathing him in, she felt his tongue softly licking into her mouth. So when he finally kicked up the heat into a full-blown soul kiss, it seemed as if they'd been kissing for hours.

Wynton wrapped one hand around the back of her neck; his thumb stroked the bone at the base of her skull, sending tingles down her spine. He'd stretched his other arm across her back and clamped onto her right butt cheek. The hard wall of his chest pressed against hers, leaving no place to put her hands except to grip his biceps.

She was just glad she had something solid to hold on to because the way he kissed her left her breathless, boneless, and mindless.

And wet.

His mouth left hers to drag kisses down the column of her throat. "If we weren't needed inside in like a minute, I'd already be inside you." He stopped and breathed heavily against her skin. "Goddammit, Melissa. What you do to me. Kissing you is ten times better than fucking most women. I don't think my brain can process how fantastic the real deal will be."

"Listen to you sweet talk me."

Wynton lifted his head. "Meet me back here in ten minutes."

Mel forced her arms to work and slid her hands across his shoulders. "I have a better idea. There's a private room for the bride to get ready around the back of the lodge." She brought his mouth down to hers for a teasing kiss. "I just happen to have a key. And a condom."

His smile lit up his whole face. "Is it too soon to say I think I love you?"

She laughed. "Save that for after I blow your...mind, cowboy."

The DJ invited all the single ladies to the dance floor for the bouquet toss.

"That's our cue."

Right before they walked into the lodge, Wynton murmured, "These next ten minutes might actually kill me, Kentucky."

"Don't worry. I know CPR. I'd revive you."

Chapter Three

Wyn watched London toss the bouquet. He thought it was telling—and maybe a little sad—that Melissa didn't even try to catch it.

Then he stood in a circle with the other guests as Sutton removed London's garter. He thought it was telling—and an indication of how smitten his younger brother was—that he refused to toss the garter and kept it for himself.

The events dragged out much longer than he'd expected and his gaze was continually drawn to Melissa. He couldn't wait to have his mouth on her skin. He couldn't wait to have those wild curls crushed in his hands. He couldn't wait to hear the noises she made as he touched her. When Cres elbowed him and muttered, "Dude. Quit eye-fucking her," Wyn actually blushed.

So what if he felt like a teenage boy locking eyes with his crush; his heart raced, sweat prickled on the back of his neck, and his dick started to harden. Melissa appeared to be in the same lustful state. Her cheeks were flushed and she alternately bit and licked her lips. The best part was when her eyes kept darting to the door.

He couldn't remember the last time he felt this level of anticipation. Maybe...never. It wasn't bragging that he didn't have to work too hard to find a hookup. Not because he was a smooth-talking Casanova. He just liked women, he liked sex, and he didn't pretend he wanted anything more than a good time.

So why haven't you gotten laid in months?

If his smartass brothers knew how long this dry spell had lasted, they'd claim it was because he'd bedded every available single woman in the area. The truth was, he'd gotten more selective after he'd watched his brother fall in love.

Finally, the newlyweds were ready to leave the reception. Cres pulled Sutton's truck up to the entrance. Earlier, they'd decorated it with dozens of tin cans and beer cans tied to the tailgate and dragging on the ground. They'd written "Just Married" along both sides in huge white letters. They'd filled the inside with rolls of toilet paper and paper streamers. Cres had even tracked down an old pamphlet "What To Expect On Your Wedding Night" and taped it to the steering wheel. But Wyn's favorite part was the two-dozen rainbow-colored condom packages he'd affixed to the hood in the shape of a bow.

As soon as the happy couple pulled away, Melissa was beside him. "Did you save any of those fun-colored condoms?"

He faced her and smiled. "Nope. I had to special order them. Hard to find a place that carries extra small rubbers."

She laughed. "You didn't."

"I did. He'd do the same damn thing to me."

They stared at each other. Moved toward each other.

He dropped his gaze to her lips. "You have the sexiest mouth I've ever seen."

"It's yours. However you want it." Her soft fingers circled his wrist. "We're doing this now?"

"Unless you've changed your mind?"

Melissa brought his hand to her mouth and sucked on his pinkie. "Does that *seem* like I've changed my mind?"

"Christ. Give me the key to the room."

She took two steps backward and an evil smile curled her lips. "Now…Where *did* I put that key? It's on me someplace. Guess you'll have to pat me down or feel me up to find it." She disappeared around the corner.

Wyn followed half a step behind her and he was on her, pushing her up against the door as his mouth crashed down on hers, kissing her with hunger and desperation that seemed totally foreign to him. His hands landed on her hips and he flattened his palms over her abdomen, traveling up her ribcage. Then he cupped her tits, sliding his fingers across the top of the dress and pulling the material away from her skin so he could reach into her cleavage.

Score. The pad of his finger brushed a metal ring.

Rather than scooping it out that way, he broke the kiss to bury his face between her breasts. Licking those full swells of flesh, inhaling the scent of her skin, snagging the key ring with his teeth and pulling it out.

"My, what a talented tongue you have, Super Man-Slut," she said breathlessly.

He grinned and the key dropped into his hand. Snaking his left arm around her waist, he yanked her against his body and jammed the key in the lock. The door popped open.

Once they were inside, he gave the place a cursory look. A single lamp lit the entire room. Three folding chairs were spread out in a semicircle, a low countertop and mirror took up one wall, and a loveseat had been shoved in the corner. Good enough.

He slammed the door and pressed her against it, fusing his mouth to hers again.

She tasted sweet. Like juice and wedding cake. He kissed her until he felt drunk just from the pleasure of it. His hands roved over as much of her as possible, but he needed more.

Wyn ran his hand up her spine until he found the zipper tab at the top of her dress and eased it down to the small of her back.

Melissa broke the kiss on a gasp. "Thank heaven. Now I can breathe."

"Pull the fabric down to your waist," he murmured against her throat.

Hooking her fingers into the side panels, she shimmied it down, baring her tits completely. "The bra is built in—"

Whatever she'd been about to say was lost in a soft moan as he dragged his fingertips over the upper curve of her breast. He locked his gaze to hers. "You want pretty words? Or you want my mouth sucking you here"—he swept his thumb across her nipple—"until I get your pussy wet enough to fuck?"

"That. Yes. Please."

Wyn palmed and caressed her while he feasted on her nipples. When her squirming forced him to release that rigid tip before he was ready, he said, "Hands above your head, gripping the top of the door frame."

She complied with barely a whimper of protest.

His dick was so damn hard it hurt. He didn't have to drag this out, but that's partially why he wanted to; she wouldn't expect it.

So he sucked and bit and licked her tits, even gifting her with a suck mark on the fleshy outer edge that nearly sent her through the roof.

His mouth drifted back up to her ear. "Do I fuck you sitting down or standing up? Choose."

"Standing up."

Wyn pulled a condom out of his pocket, holding it to her mouth with a husky, "Hang on to this for a sec."

How fucking sexy was it to see her teeth sinking into the plastic. He undid his suit pants, shoving them and his boxer briefs to his knees. He took the condom from her mouth with his own. Then he ripped the package with his teeth and reached down to roll it on.

That's when he noticed Melissa's hands were still above the door. Her chest was heaving. Her eyes...Christ her eyes were heavy-lidded and expectant.

The satiny fabric of her dress brushed against his bare thighs as he lifted the material up and tucked it behind her. He inched his fingers down until the tips connected with the waistband of her panties. "Hold still." As he pulled the panties down her trembling thighs, he crouched slightly, needing to know her scent before he fucked her. Wyn ducked his head and placed an openmouthed kiss on the curve of her mound. "A natural redhead," he murmured against that fragrant flesh.

Once her panties were off, he pressed his body to hers again. He grabbed behind her left thigh and lifted it up to wrap around his hip. Wyn planted his mouth on hers as he aligned his cock to her wet center. He pushed in slowly the first couple of inches and then snapped his hips, filling her in one fast thrust.

Melissa's moan vibrated in his mouth. She rolled her hips forward in a signal for him to move.

Keeping one hand around her thigh, he slid his other hand up her arm, pulling it away from the wall and setting it on his shoulder. He flattened his palm above her head on the door to brace himself as he started to fuck her.

The slow, steady pace didn't last long, even when he wanted to savor every glide of his cock into her tight, wet heat. But as the sensations built, he sped up.

The kiss had become frantic—thrusting tongues and hot, fast breath exchanged in openmouthed kisses.

When he kicked up the pace again, Melissa let her head fall back, leaving her neck wide open.

He nipped and nuzzled. Used his teeth. Lost his mind whenever she released a throaty sigh when his tongue connected with a hot spot. His cock rammed into her faster and harder, but he kept his mouth gentle. If he didn't consciously think about it, he feared he'd turn into an animal, leaving bite marks and broken flesh in his wake.

"Wynton."

"So fucking perfect, how you feel around me."

"I'm close," she panted.

"Tell me what'll get you there."

"Move side to side. Yes. Like that." She groaned. "Don't stop."

His grip tightened on her thigh. "Your pussy's squeezing me like a fucking vise. Take it baby, it's right. There."

That did it. She began to come immediately, her body bucking and grinding against his. The sexiest noises he'd ever heard echoed around him, taunting him to join her. But he gritted his teeth and waited until the last pulse pulled at his cock and she slumped against the wall.

Wyn couldn't hold off. Six hard strokes later, he buried his face in the curve of her neck, his hips pumping as his cock erupted.

Her lips in his hair roused him. He raised his head and feathered his mouth over hers. "That was… Hell, I'm pretty sure we *are* super fucking heroes."

She smiled.

"I don't want that to be it for tonight, Melissa."

Her eyes clouded.

"What?"

"Let's see how the rest of the night plays out."

"Got someone else lined up?" *I'll beat the fuck out of them if you do. Because no one is getting a taste of you. No way. No how.*

"No, and way to ask me that when your cock is still buried inside me. I promised London I'd keep an eye on the reception. Make sure people were still having fun. As soon as this ends, I'm all yours."

Wyn relaxed and slipped out of her. He lowered her leg to the floor and took his time kissing her before he forced himself to take a step back—mentally and literally—to get dressed and remind himself he had best man duties to fulfill too.

After they exited the room, Wyn slung his arm over her shoulder. "I could use a drink. How about you?"

"I have to drop off the key so we're not tempted to misuse the ready room again." She gave him a smug smile. "And then I'll meet you inside on the dance floor."

* * * *

Wyn had knocked back a couple of celebratory shots with Cres and Sutton's coworkers, when Melissa appeared a half hour after they'd parted ways.

"Is everything all right?"

"I had a few things to do that I'd forgotten about. Why?"

"I would've tracked you down if you'd tried to turn this into a fuck and run encounter."

She hip-checked him. "You rocked my world, Wynton Grant. I'm ready for more."

A Pitbull song started and she grabbed his hand. "You didn't think they'd play only country music tonight?"

"I could hope."

* * * *

Two songs later, Wyn and Melissa were leaving the dance floor when he saw his dad stumble back. Then he clutched the left side of his body and hit the floor. Wyn's mother, always the picture of calm, screamed and froze in place.

Wyn raced across the dance floor. That last shot of tequila threatened to come back up when he noticed the ashen tone his father's face had taken. And the fear in his dad's eyes sent Wyn's alarm bells ringing louder.

"Dad? Can you hear me?"

He nodded.

"Stay still. We'll get you some help."

By that time Cres was next to him, as well as Mick, one of the guys Sutton worked with at the gun range.

Mick said, "I have medical training. Let's focus on slow and steady breathing until the ambulance arrives."

Jim Grant nodded.

Then Mick glanced at Cres. "Can you deal with your mother please?"

"Of course."

"Stay with me, Jim," Mick said soothingly.

Wyn listened while Mick asked basic questions that didn't require more than a nod or a head shake. He vaguely heard Melissa advising guests to return to their tables because everything was under control.

It seemed like an hour passed before the EMTs arrived. Wyn pushed to his feet and looked around while medical personnel assessed his father. He sidestepped them and moved to stand beside his mother and Cres.

"What's going on?" his mother demanded. "Is it a stroke? A heart attack?"

"I don't know. They'll get him stabilized enough to hand him off to the docs in the emergency room."

"How far is the hospital from here?"

London's mother, Berlin, stepped into the circle. "About twenty minutes. The staff is top notch. But if the issue is out of their level of expertise, they'll Life Flight him to Denver." She slipped her arm around his mom's shoulder. "Take a deep breath, Sue. We don't need you passing out too."

The EMT interrupted. "Is anyone riding in the ambulance with him?"

"I am," Wyn said and took his mother's hand. "Cres and I have both been drinking so we can't drive to the hospital. You haven't. So I'll need you to drive Cres so we have a vehicle there, okay?"

She blew out a breath. "Okay." Then she turned to Berlin. "Could you—"

"Chuck and I will handle everything here as far as explaining to the guests. No worries."

"Thank you."

Wyn walked alongside the rolling stretcher, his entire focus on his father. Although he had been drinking, the instant they closed the ambulance doors, he was stone-cold sober.

* * * *

As soon as they were through the emergency room doors, the medical team whisked his father off, leaving Wyn to wait for the rest of his family to arrive. He couldn't fill out anything regarding his dad's medical history. That helpless feeling he'd experienced riding in the ambulance expanded. He'd watched in near shock as his dad had become completely unresponsive. His skin had turned the same gray color as his hair. And beneath the oxygen mask he wore, Wyn thought his lips looked blue.

He paced in the waiting room for a good thirty minutes before other family members arrived.

His mother seemed calmer. The staff immediately took her back beyond the swinging doors, leaving him and Cres alone.

"How is he?" Cres asked.

"He was unconscious the entire way here."

"They give you any indication of what might've happened?"

"I overheard heart attack when the EMT was on the police scanner."

Cres removed his suit jacket, then his bolo tie. He unbuttoned the top two buttons on his white dress shirt and rolled up the sleeves.

"How was Mom?" Wyn asked.

"Doin' that freaky-quiet Mom thing. I suspect Dad's siblings will show up within the next hour. They caught me on the way out and asked which hospital. I explained we were lucky there was even one this far out. They just don't get it."

Wyn sighed. His dad's family hadn't understood why he'd left California and used his inheritance to buy a cattle ranch in rural Colorado. And the times the Grant family had visited their relatives in Santa Ana, they didn't understand why anyone would choose to live among so many people. But despite their differences, they remained close.

Several long minutes of silence passed between Wyn and his brother, which wasn't unusual since they worked together and didn't yammer on from sunup to sundown. When Wyn glanced at the clock he was surprised to see thirty minutes had gone by.

The emergency doors opened and a whole mass of people walked in. His uncle Bill and his wife Barbie, his aunt Marie and her husband Roger. Cousin April and her husband Craig. Plus Ramsey, Sutton's boss from the gun range, Mick, and Melissa.

Uncle Bill approached first. "Any word?"

"No. They let Mom go back there as soon as she got here."

"That's good," Uncle Bill said, absentmindedly patting Wyn's shoulder.

"It was great of all of you to come, but you don't have to stick around. Cres and I can call you with updates."

"Nonsense. You boys don't need to deal with all of this yourselves. We're here. Besides, the forty years I spent as a nurse will come in handy," Aunt Marie said.

"She has a point, Wyn," Cres said.

"It'll likely be another hour at least before you know anything, so maybe we could all do with a cup of coffee to keep us alert." She signaled to her husband, daughter, and son-in-law to accompany her to the beverage station.

Ramsey moved in. "I'm assuming you haven't called the groom on his wedding night and let him know what's up?"

Wyn shook his head. "No sense in disturbing him when we don't know a damn thing about what's goin' on."

"We're heading back to the hotel. So if anything changes and you need someone to wake up the bride and groom, just call me and I'll knock on their door."

They exchanged numbers.

As Ramsey and his head instructor walked away, Wyn caught Cres looking at Mick with regret. He leaned over and murmured, "So much for your post-wedding hookup tonight, huh?"

"Fuck off."

"Is that the kind of guy you go for?" Wyn asked. Since Cres had come out to his family, they'd avoided talking about their sexual conquests. But when Wyn thought back, any talk of hookups had always come from him, not his brother.

So it shocked the hell out of him when Cres said, "The dude's a cowboy. A hot cowboy. A hot military cowboy. He knows his way around guns and he knows how to ride."

"Point taken. I'd probably wanna tap that if I swung that way."

"Christ. I cannot *believe* we're havin' this conversation." Cres snorted. "Speaking of hookups..."

Melissa wandered over. And Wyn didn't pretend he wasn't checking her out. Her dress wasn't excessively wrinkled from their smokin' hot encounter. He smirked, knowing she had a suck mark on the inside of her right breast. His gaze moved up to her lips. Oh, hell yeah. Her mouth was smooth and plump from the insane amount of time they'd spent kissing. When his eyes connected with hers, that spark of desire remained.

"How are you doing?"

"As well as can be expected without knowing anything," Wyn said. "I'm surprised to see you here." Shit. That'd come out wrong. "I mean—"

"I know what you meant, Wynton. I had your family members follow me here since I've been to this hospital a number of times."

"You were okay to drive?" Cres asked. "I swear I saw you knocking them back too."

Melissa shook her head. "Sleight of hand. I avoid things that put my judgment into question. Alcohol certainly does that."

"Amen, sister." Cres stood and stepped right in front of him. "I need caffeine. You want a cup of coffee, *Wynton?*"

Since Melissa couldn't see him, Wyn mouthed "fuck off" at the snarky way Cres enunciated his full name. "I'm fine."

"Suit yourself." Cres lumbered off.

Melissa plopped down beside him. "Did I interrupt something?"

"Nah. We're both a little punchy."

"I imagine."

He braced his forearms on his thighs. "So you weren't drinking tonight? Or you don't drink ever?"

"I did the champagne toast, but that's it. I drank sparkling water with lime or juice the rest of the night. I've learned if you don't want people to catch on to the fact you're not drinking, then don't talk about it and no one notices."

"But London said you guys were gonna do tequila shots."

"*London* did a tequila shot. I reminded her that me and tequila were on a permanent break."

Wyn smiled. "Gotcha." His smile dried. "I want you to know I was sober when we locked ourselves in that ready room."

"I know or I wouldn't have gone with you."

He reached out and brushed a few stray hairs from her cheek. "You are so freakin' sexy. I'd planned on takin' you back to my hotel room tonight—"

The doors to the back of the hospital opened.

His grim-faced mother was followed out by a man wearing a white coat and a stethoscope.

Wyn's stomach churned. He rose to his feet and Cres was instantly beside him. "Mom? What's goin' on?"

"Dr. Poole will explain."

"Bluntly put," Dr. Poole started, "Mr. Grant suffered a heart attack. To what extent the damage is, we're not sure yet. I've ordered blood tests that measure levels of cardiac enzymes, which indicate heart muscle damage."

"Whoa. You can tell that with a blood test?" Cres asked skeptically.

"Yes. The enzymes normally found inside the cells of the heart are needed for that specific organ. When the heart muscle cells are injured, their contents—including those enzymes—are released into the bloodstream, making it a testable entity."

"Thanks for the explanation," Wyn said. "What else?"

"After discussing the symptoms with Mrs. Grant, I suspect Mr. Grant's heart attack started before he hit the dance floor. We know the heart attack was still ongoing when they brought him in here. We immediately medicated him."

"But?"

"But the medicines aren't working so he's been sent to the cardiac cath lab."

All this medical terminology was making his head hurt. "What's that?"

"A cardiac catheter can be used to directly visualize the blocked artery and help us determine which procedure is needed to treat the blockage."

"You're telling us this because you've made the determination there is a significant blockage?" Wyn asked.

Dr. Poole nodded. "Once Mr. Grant has been stabilized, we'll send him to Denver, via ambulance."

"Not medevac'ing him now?

"No."

"That means...it's not that serious?" Cres asked.

"Oh, it's serious. But given that he was brought here immediately, if we observe him overnight, we'll have a full assessment to give the cardiac team in Denver tomorrow, which will save time."

"But by keeping him here and not sending him to a cardiac hospital, you're not takin' unnecessary chances with his life? 'Cause I ain't down with that at all, doc."

"Wynton," his mother softly chastised.

"I'm with Wyn on this, Mom," Cres inserted. "If Dad needs to be in Denver, fire up the helicopter and get him there. Pronto."

"I understand your concerns," Dr. Poole said. "And you have every right to question my recommendation. But I spent a decade in the cardiac unit in Salt Lake City, so I am more qualified than your average country doc."

That gave Wyn a tiny measure of relief. "Okay."

"Any other questions?"

"Can we see him?" Cres asked.

"Not right now. We'll see how the night progresses. It's up to your mother whether she stays back there with him or out here with you all."

Sue Grant lifted her chin. "My husband has suffered a major health trauma. Of course I'm staying with him." She stepped forward and offered Wyn and Cres each a hug. "As soon as I have any news, I promise I'll be out here to tell you."

Then she and Dr. Poole walked back through the swinging doors.

Wyn turned around and searched for Aunt Marie. "Did you catch all of that?"

"Yes. From the sounds of it, Jim will be out for the rest of the night. And since there's no reason for us all to be exhausted tomorrow, we'll head back to the hotel. But I promise we'll be back first thing in the morning." Her gaze winged between Wyn and Cres. "I don't suppose I can convince either of you to return to the hotel and get some rest?"

They both said "no" at the same time.

"That's what I thought." She, too, gave them both a hug. "Any change, you call me." She pulled a deck of cards out of her purse. "To pass the time."

Wyn kissed her cheek. "Thank you. You sure you're okay to drive?"

"Sober as a judge, my boy." Her brown eyes narrowed. "Last question. What about Sutton?"

"What about him?"

"He deserves to know his father is in the hospital."

"He deserves a wedding night with his wife," Wyn retorted.

"So you're suggesting we don't tell him that Dad is in the ER and headed for Denver tomorrow, possibly for surgery?" Cres demanded.

"That's exactly what I'm sayin'."

"But—"

"End of discussion, Cres."

Arguments started—and all seemed to be directed at him. So Wyn tuned them out and wandered over to the window.

He'd glared at the juniper bushes lining the sidewalk for several minutes when he felt a soft touch on his arm. He saw Melissa's reflection in the window. "What?"

"You have to tell Sutton about your dad being in the hospital, Wynton. It's his decision whether he leaves on his honeymoon tomorrow or stays here, not yours. By not telling him, you're making it *your* decision. That's not fair to him, to you, or to your father. If something unforeseen happens, and Sutton returns home to the worst news imaginable...he'll blame you for a multitude of things—starting with him not getting to say good-bye. That's too deep a burden for you to undertake."

"Do you have any idea how much this honeymoon means to my brother?" For months, Sutton had planned the four-week getaway in the tropics. Wasn't out of sight, out of mind better in this instance? Would Sutton even be able to relax and enjoy this special time with London if he was constantly calling home to check on Dad?

"I'd venture a guess...it doesn't mean as much to him as your father does."

"Jesus, Melissa."

"You need someone to be the bad guy and you don't want it to be you. But by letting Sutton know what happened and giving him the choice of what to do next, you are doing the right thing."

"It doesn't feel that way."

"I know." She swept her hand across his shoulders. "But trust me because I speak from personal experience, not telling Sutton is worse."

Wyn turned and looked at her. "This happened to you?"

"My sister had an accident while I was at camp. And instead of bringing me home, my parents let me finish out the full two weeks. We weren't allowed to have cell phones, so I didn't have a clue she almost died until after my dad picked me up. And naturally, my sister thought I wasn't there because my training camp was more important than her. It was ugly."

Before he could ask what kind of accident, Cres strolled up.

"You done bein' unreasonable?"

"Yeah."

"So you're in agreement that Sutton needs to be told?"

"Can we do it early in the morning? And at least give him the rest of this night with London? The doc pretty much told us nothin' will change tonight anyway."

"Makes sense. You cool with Aunt Marie bein' the one who knocks on the honeymoon suite door at six a.m. and tells him what's up?"

"That'd be best. He won't punch her. And she does have that calming nurse demeanor."

Right then, Aunt Marie yelled at the receptionist.

"On second thought..."

Cres chuckled. "She seems feistier than usual. I'll walk them out." Cres headed to the desk.

Melissa squeezed Wyn's arm. "She followed me here, do you want me to lead them back to the hotel?"

"If you wanna go, that's fine."

"That's not what I asked."

Wyn studied her. "Why would you want to stay? We just met today. For all you know I could be a total dick."

"A total dick usually doesn't know he's a total dick, so that argument doesn't apply. Try again."

"Do you *want* to stay?"

"Yes."

He exhaled. "Good. Because to be honest, I didn't know how to ask you to stay. This is"—he gestured to the hospital and to her—"screwing with my head."

She stood on tiptoe to whisper, "I'd rather be screwing with your body, but since that's not in the cards..." Then she stepped back and pointed to his hand. "Speaking of cards...playing strip poker would be a great way to kill time."

"Strip poker, huh?"

"Virtual strip poker, beings we're in public."

"How's that work?"

"We keep score. The next time we're alone together, we'll have a specific order in how we remove our clothes."

For the first time in two hours he had a sense of hope about something—it sounded like Melissa didn't want this thing with them to be a one and done either. "You keep score, baby, and I'll deal the first hand."

Chapter Four

Mel laid down her cards. "Full house, jacks over sevens."

"Damn. I thought I had you this time." Wynton spread out three twos, a six, and a ten.

"Three of a kind with deuces?" she tsk-tsked. "With two players that's never a good gamble." She eyed his shirt collar and imagined peeling that pristine white shirt off his broad shoulders and down his muscular arms. Her gaze caught on the thick column of his neck. She wanted to sink her teeth into that hard flesh. Taste the salt and musk on his skin. Fill her senses with the overpowering maleness of him.

"Melissa, darlin'? You okay?"

Her focus snapped back to him. "I'm fine. Why?"

"You moaned like you were in pain."

She leaned forward. "That moan was your fault. See, I imagined stripping you out of that pesky shirt and my mind wandered south from there."

"You're already kicking my ass at poker and now you gotta give me a hard-on in the waiting room?"

"Just keeping you updated on how eager I am to get my greedy hands all over your naked body. You had way too many clothes on before."

"The feeling is mutual."

But he was distracted when he said that so Melissa turned toward the front entrance when he muttered, "I'll be damned."

The good-looking military guy who'd first offered Jim medical assistance at the wedding paused inside the doors and scanned the waiting area. At the end of the row, Cres straightened up and ran his hand over his hair before he stood.

The guy saw him and smiled. Cres met him halfway and they shook hands, but not in the usual way guys shook hands. Their connection lingered.

Holy crap. Cres Grant was gay.

She sent a sidelong glance at Wynton. Did he know?

He watched the two men, not exactly circumspectly, as he shuffled the deck.

"Is that a friend of your brother's? I saw them talking at the wedding. And he left with Sutton's boss when I got here. Think he came back to see how your dad's doing?"

Wynton said nothing but then she felt him staring at her.

When their eyes met, she got her answer—wariness. Like he was afraid she'd pass judgment on his brother.

As if.

Other people's sexual preferences weren't her concern—she had enough issues with her own sexual needs to worry about someone else's. "How long have you known that Cres is...?"

"Gay?" he said softly. "He came out to us last year. Right after Sutton and London got engaged." His eyes narrowed. "But it's not common knowledge."

"Those two keep looking at each other like that in public and it will be," Mel said dryly. She picked up her cards without really looking at them. "I'd never take it upon myself to point out the obvious to others who can't see it."

"Thank God for that."

"Were you surprised when he came out?"

"Honestly? Yeah. I guess the signs were there if I cared to look. He hadn't had a serious girlfriend...ever really. Hadn't dated any girl since high school. He didn't like trolling the bars with me. Even before I hit pause on my libido last year, he preferred that we hang out and play video games on the weekends."

What did he mean...*hit pause on his libido*?

"And he always did love men's wrestling a little too much."

Mel's gaze snapped to his. "Seriously?"

He smirked. "Nah. Just seein' if you're paying attention."

"Jerk." She tossed her cards down. "This hand is crap. Re-deal."

Wynton shuffled again. Surprisingly, he kept talking. "As an adult, Cres has always seemed preoccupied. When I think back...I just wish he would've told us sooner. Because right after he told us, it was as if a giant weight had been lifted from him. I hated that he carried that weight at all."

You sweet, thoughtful man. He was a good brother—did *his* brothers appreciate that? "So your family is fine with everything?"

"Cres has always been tight-lipped. But like I said, it filled in some of the pieces about Cres that hadn't fit before. So he's got our acceptance, and I think that's all that really worried him. Who else he chooses to tell ain't my concern. It sure as hell ain't my business who he dates. I'm just happy he can be himself and date who he wants."

Mel held her fist out for a bump. "Amen. I'll just throw it out there that we wouldn't be having this conversation if Cres was on the rodeo circuit. If there's even a whisper of that kind of relationship, they're unofficially blackballed."

"That's what Sutton said too." Wynton dealt them each a new hand. "So tell me about your sister. You said she had an accident. What happened?"

How did she explain this? The few times she'd bothered, she worried she'd come off sounding like a poor little rich girl or resentful, which wasn't the case. So she usually avoided the topic entirely with men by just dropping to her knees.

A rough-skinned hand skated up her arm. "With all that we've been through today, I hope you won't start holdin' back on me now."

She inhaled a deep breath and let it all spill out. "My parents are loaded, okay? One of those requirements of being a Lockhart was making sure I excelled at riding, horsemanship, dressage, the whole package. The camp I attended when my sister Alyssa was injured was an exclusive, by-invitation-only camp at a training facility for Olympic athletes. The best trainers in the world were there. So in my parent's eyes, pulling me from camp would've been viewed in the same horrifying light as dropping out of the program because I couldn't cut it. And the Lockharts couldn't have anyone believing that of them or their human progeny." She closed her eyes. The ache of that time had lessened but hadn't disappeared completely.

Wynton cupped her jaw in his hand and lifted her face to his. "Hey. If it bothers you too much to tell me—"

"It doesn't. I just haven't talked about it in a while."

"Then I'm flattered you're sharing all this with me."

"Anyway, throughout my entire life I'd been groomed to win the gold medal in the Olympics while riding a Lockhart horse, thereby increasing its worth and mine."

"Harsh assessment, baby."

"But it's true."

"How old is your sister?"

"Alyssa is six years younger than me."

"What happened?"

"She was at a birthday party. There were go-cart races and she crashed through a fence. The fence crushed her legs and she ended up paralyzed from the waist down."

His jaw dropped to the floor. After he picked it up, he said, "Keep goin'."

"My parents focused completely on my sister—as they should have. Alyssa was really awful after the accident. She especially hated the sight of me. She resented me. Not solely because I wasn't by her side immediately after the accident, but because I was…whole, if that makes sense. As accomplished a horsewoman that I was, Alyssa was better. I'd always known if I'd failed to meet my parent's expectations, the Lockharts had another shot of having an Olympian in the family with Alyssa. I stopped riding and training after her accident because I wanted to be there for her. But she didn't want me anywhere near her. After enduring two solid months of her screaming at me to get the hell away from her, the doctors and my parents asked me to stop coming to visit her, at least until she wasn't so angry. And because it was in Alyssa's best interest, I left."

Wynton picked up her hand and kissed the inside of her wrist.

"So while my sister recovered from a near-fatal accident, I reset my priorities."

"Ran away with the rodeo, did you?"

She smiled. "Something like that. I continued to check on her, but since I was out of sight, I wasn't on my parents' minds. And don't think I was resentful because I wasn't. I was an adult. Alyssa needed them so much more than I did."

"Did your sister come around? Stop resenting you?"

"Yes. I never held the way she acted against her because she suffered a horrible life-altering ordeal at such a young age. Eventually we mended all fences. But I had no interest in going back to that world and competing on the level I'd been at before her accident. After two years, Alyssa set her mind to competing again. She trained for the Paralympics and won several national equestrian championships. She's competed in the international Paralympics, winning a silver and a bronze medal. She's so determined to succeed for herself—not just for our parents—that she won't quit until she's won a gold medal. I'm so proud of her. She's turned out to be an inspiration to so many people."

"I wish I had your attitude. I'm ashamed to say I didn't. Not either time Sutton was injured. The second time I was so mad at him when he opted to go back into rodeo. It seemed selfish of him to continue. And when he was in the hospital, I stayed away. I claimed I had extra ranch work to do because Dad was at Sutton's side, but that wasn't the reason. I just couldn't handle seein' my brother like that. I don't do well when it comes to illnesses and hospitals."

She experienced that familiar punch of sadness. She'd heard that so many times—not only over the last six months, but whenever she talked about her sister's struggles. She'd walked away for her sister's benefit—not because she couldn't deal with it. Now their relationship was solid, but she hadn't even considered calling Alyssa when she'd gotten her diagnosis—especially not after how their mother had reacted when she'd finally told her.

"Hey, Kentucky, where'd you go?" he said softly.

Mel returned her focus to him. The man had the most expressive face. More rugged than handsome, if she had to put a name to it. His features weren't as sharply defined as either of his brother's—Sutton Grant defined gorgeous and Cres Grant was almost pretty—but Wynton's raw-boned features gave him an equally striking look. His hair, in the vivid brightness of the fluorescent lights, held a dark red hue, which made the pieces curling around his ears more boyish looking.

"Darlin', you keep lookin' at me like that and I'm gonna start searching for a supply closet."

"Don't toss out suggestions you won't follow through with," she said.

He cocked a dark eyebrow. "Why don't you think I'll follow through?"

She threaded her fingers through his. "Because even with all this flirty and sexy banter, and me trying to convey my complicated past to try and take your mind off the present, I see the strain in your eyes. You're worried about your dad. But you're also worried about your mom. You feel guilty that you have someone out here with you—even if I wasn't here you'd still have Cres to kill time with—whereas your mother is back there alone."

"You caught all that?" He paused, brooding look in place. "What else?"

"I figured you'd play another two hands of poker with me, letting me believe I was successful at distracting you, before you wandered to the front desk to see if you could go back there and check on your mother, or try to get some kind of message to her to see how she's doing."

"How do you do that?"

"What?"

"Read my mind. It's a little spooky."

"Why?"

He frowned. "Because we've only known each other for a few hours."

But I've known about you for almost a year. The man London claimed had sadness behind his perpetual smile. The man who used sex to combat loneliness, just like I do. The man I refused to let my best friend set me up with—and yet somehow, she did it anyway, without even knowing it.

"Melissa?"

She glanced up from staring at his hard-skinned knuckles. "But in those few hours we've fucked, swapped life stories, and shared some brutal truths, so we're beyond the 'what's your favorite movie?' first date type of bullshit." She brought his hand to her mouth. "So go do what you have to. I'll hang around in the off chance I can continue to be a distraction."

He kissed her. "Thank you. I'll be back."

* * * *

While Wynton was in the back with his mother, Mel did a little exploring. The hospital wasn't very big and most of the private areas were in the back beyond the swinging doors, so that put a wrinkle in her plan.

When Wynton appeared about fifteen minutes later, Mel couldn't help but watch him saunter toward her—his tall, muscular body a visual feast even covered in clothes. He exuded confidence, despite the worry wrinkling his brow, and it made her realize all the guys she'd been playing around with were just boys compared to this man.

Cres intercepted him before he reached the sitting area, and she tried to decipher their grim conversation. Cres nodded, clapped Wynton on the shoulder and stepped aside.

Then Wynton's eyes met hers and she was on her feet by the time he stood in front of her. "No change."

"Sorry." She touched his cheek. "You look like you could use some fresh air."

"That I could." He squinted at the thin wrap covering her shoulders and shrugged out of his suit jacket. "Needing to clear my head don't mean I want you to freeze, darlin'." He draped the coat around her.

His scent enveloped her and his gesture warmed her more than the actual coat. "Thanks."

"Let's take a walk." They exited through the emergency room doors and paused outside the building. The October air had a sharp bite. When Wynton exhaled, she saw some of the tension leave his shoulders. The rancher definitely didn't like to be cooped up.

He dropped his arm across her shoulders and pulled her close so he could kiss her temple. "If I haven't said it enough, I appreciate you bein' here, Melissa."

The security lights lit the sidewalk as they walked around the building. They didn't speak, but the silence didn't seem forced or awkward.

When they reached the edge of the parking lot, Mel said, "My coat is in the car and I'd really love to change out of these shoes."

"Of course."

She hit the unlock button on the Jeep Cherokee and skirted the front end to slide into the driver's side. Wynton slipped into the passenger's seat. She started the engine. "No need for us to sit in the cold." She felt his questioning gaze when she turned the dashboard lights off.

"This is a nice SUV," he said. "It's got enough horsepower to pull your horse trailer?"

"This isn't mine. It belongs to the Gradsky's. I borrow it when I'm not on the road." Mel twisted around to dig on the floor behind Wynton for her athletic shoes. "It gets considerably better gas mileage than my Chevy Tahoe." She kicked off her high-heeled boots and slipped her feet into athletic shoes.

"I never asked how much you're on the road?"

She skirted his question with, "Give me the play-by-play of your multiple ménages, Wynton. Girl/girl/guy?"

"Yep."

"Girl/guy/girl?"

"That too."

"What about guy/girl/guy?"

"Yep, and before you go on, never been in a guy/guy/girl threesome."

She grinned. "That's funny because that's the only type I've ever been in. And talk about scorching hot, watching the two guys together, their hands, mouths, and bodies all over each other. It was fucking powerful."

Wynton reached over and tucked a flyaway curl behind her ear. "Same thing with the girl on girl action. Those soft hands and mouths exploring all that smooth and supple skin. I still remember the sucking sounds. The feminine squeaks and sighs. Then how hot it was to have them turn all that focus on me. Only time I wish I'd had a cock and a strap-on so I could fuck them both at once."

"Put that in your spank bank, did you?"

"Hell, yeah." Even in the dark she could see his eyes glittering when he ran the back of his knuckles down her jawline. "That encounter in the ready room is gonna go in there too."

"I'm flattered." Mel turned her head and rubbed her lips across the base of his hand. "Unzip your pants and pull your cock out. I'll give you something else to file away for a future round of self-love."

Those amazing eyes of his burned black with desire. He kept his gaze locked to hers when he unbuckled his belt. When he lowered the zipper. When he lifted his hips off the seat. When he tugged his pants and his boxer briefs to his knees. Then he eased the seat back and folded his arms behind his head.

Mel dropped her gaze to his groin, not surprised to see he already sported a full-blown erection. She shifted in her seat, angling forward across the console. Bracing one hand on his muscular thigh and the other on his chest, she parted her lips—after kissing the head—and let that hard satin heat pass over her teeth and tongue. She held her breath through the gag reflex when the tip connected with her soft palette and bumped the back of her throat.

Wynton made an inarticulate moan.

Encouraged, she started the long glide up and down his thick shaft, the wetness in her mouth easing her way, each pass progressively lower until she was deep-throating him every time. She didn't use her hands. Just the wet heat of her mouth, the sassy flick of her tongue, and the suctioning power of her cheeks.

She shouldn't have been surprised when his hand landed on the top of her head and held her in place the moment his cock was buried deep. Her eyes watered and her pulse whooshed in her ears, but she still heard him say, "That's it, baby. Take it all. Now swallow. Fuck, yeah. Do that again."

She did what he asked because she had no problem taking direction—except when she didn't. But this wasn't one of those times. And she didn't intend to tease and drag this out. She knew they didn't have much time, so she'd make this fast.

"You could own me with this mouth," he said gruffly when she began bobbing her head, using shallower strokes and stopping to suckle on the tip.

The heater finally kicked out some warmth, turning the inside of the car sultry.

Mel felt that rush of primal satisfaction when he started to pump his hips up to meet the downward motion of her mouth. His grip tightened in her hair. He muttered something about her never fucking stopping when she earned her reward.

His cock got harder yet. In the next instant, it jerked against the roof of her mouth in hot bursts, sending his seed flowing down the back of her throat. She swallowed repeatedly, the mantra in her head *gimme, gimme, gimme* as he shot his load until he had nothing left.

Even when Wynton attempted to pull her head away, she sank her teeth into the base of his cock, keeping him in place so she could suck and lick as his dick softened.

Before she released him completely, she nuzzled his pubic hair. She loved giving head. Every man reacted differently—well, they all acted grateful—but besides that, she reveled in their reaction in the aftermath. Some men wanted to kiss her and taste their come on her tongue. Some men avoided kissing her mouth entirely. Some men wanted to return the favor and practically dove between her thighs. Some men actually stared at her in awe and spent several long moments just tracing her swollen lips. Some men wanted to cuddle. The men with phenomenal recovery time were ready to fuck. So her heart raced when she glanced up to see how Wynton would act.

As soon as he had her eyes, he fisted one big hand in the front of her dress and curled his other hand around the back of her neck as his mouth crashed down on hers in a blistering kiss. He sucked her tongue hard, as if trying to take his essence back from her.

Oh. That was hot as hell.

The kiss made her dizzy and who knows how long it would've gone on if the seatbelt latch hadn't jabbed her in the side, causing her to break away.

"What? You okay?" he asked.

"It's ironic that I'm at the wrong angle now."

"There sure as hell wasn't anything wrong with the angle you were at before." He followed the upper bow of her lip with the pad of his thumb. "That was awesome. Thank you."

"Spank bank worthy?"

"Definitely."

Mel gave him one last lingering kiss before she returned to her seat so he could adjust his clothing. When she reached back for her coat, he grabbed her hand and brought it to his mouth.

"Are you wet?"

"Very."

"I could slip my hand up your dress and get you off." He kissed her palm again. "Or I could stay like this and watch you get yourself off. That'd be hot."

"It would be. But I didn't blow you because I expected something in return."

His eyes searched hers. "Why *did* you blow me? To take my mind off the family medical stuff?"

"No. I blew you because I wanted to get up close and personal with your cock."

"That's it?"

"You were expecting a more dramatic reason?"

"Maybe a more believable one."

Do not get angry. "Explain."

"In my experience, most women don't mind givin' blowjobs, but when they do it's definitely in expectation of me spending time between their thighs."

"So is eating pussy just a reciprocal thing for you?"

"Meaning I only do it when it's expected of me?" He paused and shook his head. "If I'da had my way at the reception? Before we fucked I would've been on my knees with your thigh wrapped around the back of my neck until I ate my fill of you and made you come at least twice."

Her pulse leapt at the image of Wynton's head beneath her dress and his hungry mouth showing her what he'd learned during his years as Super Man-Slut.

"I ain't proud to admit this, but I've had women blow me in hopes of getting an introduction to my world champion bulldogger brother, Sutton. I've had women blow me after an expensive dinner because they felt they owed me." He scowled. "How I kept my dick hard after hearing that is a mystery. I've had women blow me because I've asked them to put their mouths on my dick. Have I ever had a woman blow me because she just likes sucking cock and she's good at it?" Another pause, another soft kiss to the center of her palm. "No, ma'am."

Mel laughed. "Glad I'm unique and brought something new to the table."

"That you did. And while I love spending time with my cock in your mouth, I'm happier that you showed up at the hospital and have given me a chance to get to know you beyond that."

Not for the first time, Mel thought it was a shame they didn't live closer to each other because she'd like to explore this connection for longer than one night.

"We'd better go inside. I doubt anything has changed, but I need to be there in case something does."

She kissed him. "Let's go."

Chapter Five

Wyn awoke with a start when someone jostled him. Melissa immediately sat upright.

Sutton loomed over him. He didn't look pleased. London hung back behind him, covering her mouth with a yawn.

"Mornin' newlyweds."

"While I appreciate that *someone* told me the news about Dad this morning, I ain't too happy that I wasn't told last night."

"Well, excuse the fuck outta me for not wanting to interrupt your wedding night," Wyn snapped.

Cres ambled over and squared off against Sutton. "Both of you need to chill out. Nothin' has changed in the six hours that we've been here so there was no need for you to be here, okay? Mom's the only one allowed back there. We've seen her one time. We'll know more when the doctor makes rounds this morning."

"Any idea when that'll be?"

Wyn shook his head. "But even last night the doctor indicated they'd be sending Dad to Denver via ambulance. Whether they're doin' surgery or what is up in the air." He watched his brother try and get control.

Guilt and sadness crossed Sutton's face when he looked at his wife. "I hate to say this, sweetheart, but you'll have to go on the honeymoon by yourself so we don't lose the deposits. I'll catch up if—and when I can."

Beside him, Melissa sucked in a soft breath and muttered, "Wrong answer, bud."

"Go on our honeymoon by myself," London repeated. "Because that's what I care about, more than making sure your father is okay, more than making sure I'm there for you so *you're* okay, that we don't lose the fucking deposits?" London got in Sutton's face. "Let me tell you something, asshat. I am your *wife*. I am part of this family. Do you think I could just kick back on the beach with a fruity drink in my hand when your dad is fighting for his life? Do you think I'm so—"

Sutton covered her mouth in a silencing kiss. Then he said, "Point taken."

"Good. If we have to cancel the honeymoon—"

"You don't need to cancel the honeymoon," their mom said from behind them. "You might have to delay it a few days, that's all."

Wyn stood. "Mom. Sit. You look exhausted."

"I am exhausted but I've been sitting all night." She looked at each one of her sons and her daughter-in-law, giving Melissa and Mick both a quick, questioning glance before she spoke. "Dr. Poole has already been here this morning. The damage from the heart attack wasn't as bad as they'd originally believed. All that means is your dad most likely won't need surgery, but the cardiac unit in Denver will make the final determination. They'll be transporting him soon. What hasn't changed is the fact that he had a heart attack, and even if they just check him out in Denver for a day or two and then send him home, he is out of commission for at least eight weeks. Eight weeks in which he is to do nothing but recover. Not a half-assed 'I'm fine, the doctors don't know shit' kind of recovery that he *thinks* he might get away with."

Cres laughed.

"So what I need from you boys is your promise that you won't let him do diddly squat for the next two months. You won't let him get in his feed truck. You won't even let him ride along and open fences."

"Harsh, Mom."

"I have to be harsh, Wyn. I'm not going to lose that man because of his stupid pride." Her chin wobbled and Wyn wrapped an arm around her.

"We've got your back. We promise not to let him pull any crap," Cres said.

"Easier said than done because you're shipping cattle in the next two weeks," his mother said. "Yesterday, before any of this happened, your dad mentioned being shorthanded with Sutton off on his honeymoon. So you know his first response will be to climb on his horse and round up the herd to help you boys sort cattle."

"That ain't happening," Sutton said. "If you can put off shipping even for a week, we can cut the honeymoon short so I can come back and help."

Wyn shook his head. "Because of the wedding, we're starting this a week late as it is. The last thing we need is to lose all our calves to an early blizzard or freezing rain like happened in South Dakota and Wyoming last year."

"If you've got no one that can fill in for Dad, then we'll postpone the honeymoon." Sutton sent London a pleading look. "Sorry, sweetheart."

But London was studying Melissa. "Mel, what do you have going on the next couple of weeks?"

"Not much. I have a break in teaching."

"Good. Then you can help out at the Grant Ranch."

Wyn, Cres, and Sutton all said, "What?" simultaneously.

"Oh, for God's sake. Mel is a cutting horse champion. You guys all know what the main skill is for a cutting horse, right? Sorting livestock. Her horse is at my folk's farm. She can load Plato up and spend the next couple weeks in the field doing what she's trained to do."

Wyn looked at Melissa, who seemed equally shocked by the suggestion.

"London, doll, as much as I love you, you can't go offering Mel's help without askin' her first," Sutton drawled.

"You heard her. It's not like she's got other plans. And Wyn has an extra room where she can stay. So does Cres. That way your mom"—she flashed Sue a smile—"can be with your dad all the time so there's no chance he'll go against doctor's orders and jeopardize his recovery."

"That would be a huge relief to me," his mom admitted.

"Plus, not only is Mel a cutting horse champ, the past five years she's been working as part of a penning team. Shoot, I'll bet she can cut your sorting time down to nothin'. Am I right, Mel?"

All eyes zoomed to Melissa.

"About the sorting time? No. The Grant boys are ranch born. They'll ride circles around me. But if you need an extra horse and rider, I'd be happy to help out in any way that I can."

"Then it's settled," London declared. "You all can figure out where Mel is staying later."

Wyn knew exactly where she'd be staying for the next few weeks.

Everyone started talking and Wyn leaned down to speak to Melissa privately. "You really okay with this?"

"I was thinking to myself earlier that I wished you and I had more time together, and now I've got my wish." She smirked.

"What?"

"This wasn't as altruistic of London as you might believe."

He chuckled. "Yes, it *is* fortunate that they won't have to miss more than a day or two of their honeymoon, isn't it? Because the ranch matters are handled."

"That and you know she's been trying to fix us up since she and Sutton got engaged."

That took Wyn by surprise. "Then why is their wedding the first time I met you?"

Melissa looked away. "I have no idea."

Like hell. He'd find out more about that later. "The circumstances suck, but I'm glad you're staying with me."

"Me too. I'll be happy to bunk in your guest room."

"I'd rather have you in my bed, but I'll leave that up to you."

* * * *

Wyn gave Melissa his address and the key to his front door. She had a few loose ends to tie up before she made the two-and-a-half-hour trek to the Grant Ranch, and she wouldn't arrive until late tomorrow afternoon. Normally, he didn't like people in his house when he wasn't there, but she didn't feel like a stranger. He might've obsessed on that if he hadn't been obsessing on coordinating family and vehicles as they caravanned to Denver.

Before the orderlies loaded "Big" Jim Grant in the ambulance, the doctor allowed Wyn and his brothers to see their dad for a short visit. The old man looked better than he had the previous night. Sometimes Wyn forgot that his dad was in his late sixties. He didn't look his age, nor did he act it—having a heart attack while dancing to "La Bamba" pretty much summed that sentiment up perfectly.

Now they watched the ambulance pull away and Wyn felt a pang of worry again.

"Mom seemed more relaxed about all of this," Cres commented.

"She puts on a good front in front of Dad."

Wyn looked at Sutton. "I suspect you're right."

"I ain't a doctor, but if Dad's condition was a life or death matter, they would've airlifted him last night. Hospitals don't fuck around with that stuff," Sutton said.

"You would know."

London nestled her head on Sutton's chest. "We are all staying in the same place tonight?"

"Sounds like. It's within walking distance to the hospital."

Cres looked up at the grayish cast to the sky. "I'd better get. Sure hope it doesn't snow."

"I hate that you're goin' home to check cattle by yourself." This time of year and this close to shipping, the cattle couldn't be unattended for even a day. Wyn had stayed behind yesterday morning when everyone else had gone to Gradsky's to get ready for the wedding. Today, one of them had to go home and take care of the herd, and Cres had volunteered. So it'd be at least eight hours before he got to Denver.

"Mick has offered to help me, if that's all right."

Wyn looked at the deep red flush on his brother's face. This was the first time since Cres had come out that he'd shown an interest in a guy around his family. Normally, Wyn would give him a rash of shit, but this was new territory for all of them.

"That's great," Sutton answered. "Mick mentioned when we were workin' at the range that he grew up on a ranch in Montana before he joined the service."

"Yeah, so he ain't just a pretty gate opener."

Both Wyn and Sutton's jaws dropped. They said nothing. What the hell could they say?

London laughed. She dug out ten bucks, crumpled it into a ball, and tossed it at Cres. "Remind me never to bet against you." She nudged Sutton. "Cres bet me he could say something that'd leave both of you tongue-tied."

"Bettin' against me on the second day we're married, Mrs. Grant, is gonna get you in a whole passel of trouble," Sutton warned.

She murmured something to him that made him grin.

"Jesus. Can we just go already?" Wyn complained.

"Yep. See you guys later. Without bein' a dick, I hope I don't hear from you at all until I walk into the hospital in Denver," Cres said.

"Amen, brother. Drive safe."

* * * *

Late the next afternoon, Berlin Gradsky asked Mel, "Are you sure you'll be all right?"

Berlin mothered Mel way more than her own mother did. "I'll be fine. I'm actually really excited to put Plato through his paces."

"London was right about one thing. This is what Plato was trained for."

After Mel climbed in her truck, Berlin rested her forearms on the window jamb. "Nosy question."

"Hit me."

"Is there a reason why you're staying at Wyn Grant's house and not house sitting for London and Sutton while they're on their honeymoon?"

Yes, because I plan on riding Wynton Grant as hard as Plato for the next three weeks. "Sutton said something about liability issues because of his indoor gun range. I didn't question it. And given my...condition, it's probably smart."

Berlin squeezed Mel's shoulder. "No one knows, do they? Not even my daughter?"

She shook her head. "London didn't need that extra stress during her wedding planning. We both know she would've stressed about that too." But her friend wasn't dumb. She'd asked Mel several times if she was avoiding her. She'd asked if something had happened on the circuit to make Mel drop out. Mel would tell her the reason she'd been distant the last six months as soon as her bossy-pants BFF returned from her honeymoon.

"You're right. I'm happy for my daughter and son-in-law, but I'm glad the wedding is over." She smiled. "Now I just have to worry about you."

"I promise not to take any chances with Plato if I'm not feeling up to it. You know I'd never risk his safety. I'll be fine as long as I follow the rules."

"I've watched you get a handle on this, sweetie, so I trust you with him."

"Thanks for everything."

"You're welcome. Drive safe. Text me when you get there."

"I will."

Berlin stepped back and Mel slowly pulled the horse trailer down the long road leading away from Grade A Farms.

The drive to the Grant Ranch was a little over two hours, and Mel didn't have any reason to hurry. Chances were good she'd beat Wynton there. The family had been in Denver since yesterday, and today they were getting the final diagnosis on the Grant patriarch. She'd stalled as long as she could at Gradsky's. She'd even driven into town and loaded up on groceries because she wasn't sure what type of food a bachelor rancher would stock.

In the last six months, after being diagnosed with type 1 diabetes, Mel had no choice but to monitor every morsel of food that went into her mouth. She also had to reduce her physical activity because she was still learning her limits—which weren't even close to the same as they'd been before her diagnosis.

She hadn't been lucky enough to "get" type 2 diabetes, which allowed her to control her blood sugar levels with modifications to her diet. Her regulation came in the form of daily shots of insulin. Keeping snacks within reach for those times when she felt her glycemic index was low. Carrying glucose tablets with her. Making sure she always had her blood glucose meter, glucose strips, lancets, her needle disposal container, and insulin with her. Thankfully, she could inject herself with an insulin pen, and the type of insulin it used didn't have to be refrigerated.

Even after six months, she wasn't sure she'd ever get used to any of this. It still seemed surreal.

After fighting fatigue, excessive thirst, and weight loss for two months, when she was in LA she finally went to the ER because she thought she might have mono. She'd had it once before and the symptoms seemed similar. The doctor hadn't been convinced her body would react that way to the stress of being on the road, so she'd ordered a battery of tests. When the blood and urine tests had come back positive for diabetes, and further testing indicated type 1 diabetes—a rare diagnosis in a thirty-two-year-old—Mel had literally passed out.

After she'd come to in the hospital, she'd learned the meaning of diabetic shock. She learned her life would never be the same. Ironically, she'd chosen a hospital that had an entire department devoted to dealing with diabetic patients. She learned how to inject herself with insulin. She'd taken a two-day course on proper nutrition, the dangers of excessive physical activity, and how to monitor her blood sugar. She'd soaked it all in. The only time she'd outwardly balked was during her appointment with a counselor who blathered on about emotional changes affecting the body.

Mel had been numb to that. The physical changes concerned her because she realized she'd have to quit competing. It wasn't just her and her horse in the arena, like a barrel racer, or a bulldogger, or a tie down roper. No, in the cutting horse division, it was her, her horse, and ten or more cows. During team penning competition, there were two other riders on horses and up to thirty calves. In other words—mass chaos. She couldn't take the chance that she'd have a low glycemic moment and pass out on top of her horse.

Again.

It had happened to her during a competition, prior to her diagnosis. At the time she'd blamed it on excessive heat in the arena, or being overly tired. She was lucky she hadn't injured herself or someone else.

Especially since she hadn't remembered anything that had happened.

Mel had withdrawn from all competitions. She'd been in limbo, trying to figure out what to do with her life now that her life had changed. Being a trust fund baby did have some perks—she didn't have to decide immediately.

The scenery kept her interest for the remainder of the drive. When she turned down the dirt road that the GPS indicated led to Wynton's house, she envied him and this view every day. Hills and flat land and those gorgeous snow-topped Rocky Mountains in the distance.

His house wasn't what she expected. It was an older ranch house with one old barn, one enormous new barn, and loading pens off to the side of the corral. She pulled the horse trailer up to the pasture Wynton had recommended. She'd keep Plato segregated for a few days until he became acclimated to the area and the other horses.

Since she'd exercised Plato first thing this morning, she checked him for any new marks after being cooped up in the horse trailer. Sometimes the temperamental horse would kick the walls and she'd open up the back end to see him bleeding. But he didn't look worse for the wear, so she fed him and turned him loose.

The next thing Mel did was open the house and cart all of her stuff inside, dumping it in the guest bedroom. She wanted to set the parameters from day one. She couldn't wait to fuck Wynton in every way she'd fantasized about—okay, maybe she had actually written down a list of all the positions and scenarios she wanted to try with Super Man-Slut—but she would be sleeping and waking up alone every night.

You are such a chicken-shit. Why don't you just tell him the truth?

Because she didn't want to blow a good thing. Sexually, they seemed to be on the same page, and that was all that mattered.

She stowed her insulin in the back of the closet. She hid her blood sugar meter in the same drawer as the Glucagon emergency kit. She filled the nightstand drawer with her new best friend—a constant supply of snacks. Then she unpacked her clothes and put them away. She set up her laptop, her cell phone charger, and her e-reader. She spread her toiletries out on the counter in the bathroom across the hallway, including the brand new, unopened jumbo-sized box of condoms.

Then she allowed herself to explore.

Wynton's house was a four-bedroom ranch with a decent-sized living room, and a kitchen that opened into the dining room. Off the dining room was a patio that was completely enclosed by an eight-foot tall fence. The space was homey, although a few things didn't fit. Like the rooster-imaged ruffled curtains in the kitchen and the peach-colored walls in the living room. But the gigantic TV and gaming system, and the oversized recliners and couch did scream bachelor.

One place she didn't even peek into was the closed door at the opposite end of the hallway from her room. It seemed...intrusive to check out Wynton's bedroom when he wasn't here.

And since she had no idea what time he'd arrive, she carried in the groceries she'd packed in the cooler and took stock of his pantry. Good thing she stopped at the store.

Mel had just finished the chicken stir-fry when she heard the front door open.

* * * *

The wait for the doctor's diagnosis today had been nerve-racking. But the good news had been such a relief. His dad had a new diet and exercise regimen. He had eight weeks off to recover because he would make a full recovery.

Before they'd had a chance to celebrate, Jim Grant had announced to his family that he intended to retire from ranching entirely. Starting immediately. Then he'd given Wyn and Cres the option of dividing the land in half. They could each run their own operation, or they could continue to ranch together. He'd take his cut of the cattle sale from this year and then after that, he was out. He planned to fulfill his promise to his wife to see the world. And as soon as he was healthy enough, they'd be off to have the adventures they'd waited a lifetime to experience.

Talk about floored.

Wyn was glad to have several hours to try to sort through everything. But by the time he pulled into his driveway just after dark, he was more than ready to put it all aside and focus on the sweet, hot and sexy redhead he hadn't been able to get out of his mind the past thirty-six hours. The sweet, hot and sexy redhead who was in his house right now. The sweet, hot and sexy redhead who had left the porch light on for him.

Warmth spread through him. It made him a fucking sap, but he hadn't had anyone leave the light on for him since he lived at home. And if the woman had cooked supper? He might just propose to her.

He was so eager to see her he didn't haul in his suitcase. He took the steps two at a time and burst through the door. From the foyer, while he took off his boots, he yelled, "Honey, I'm home." When he rounded the corner, Melissa stood in his living room, her wild curls pulled back into a ponytail. She wore a workout top that showcased her tits, yoga pants—thank you baby Jesus for the genius who invented *those* motherfuckers—and her feet were bare. She looked completely at home in his home.

"Hey. How was the drive?"

"Long."

"How's your dad?"

"Better than we thought, on the road to a full recovery and makin' big plans." He started to stalk her. "Tell me, little redheaded riding girl, what's that delicious smell?"

"I cooked stir-fry but the rice isn't done yet."

"Good. We have time."

Melissa took a step back. "For?"

"For you to tell me why you were trespassing in my kitchen."

"Are you the big bad wolf, Wynton?"

"Yes." He continued slowly moving forward. "Here's where you say, 'Oh my, what big teeth you have.'"

Her gaze zeroed in on his mouth. "Why are you licking your lips?"

"Because you look mighty tasty."

"But I cooked!"

"Don't want food, Red. I want you." Then he was looming over her. The sexy glint in her eyes widened his predatory grin. "Strip off them britches."

Her half-hearted "No" had him wrestling her to the floor. He hovered on all fours above her. "Don't be scared, Red. My big teeth and long wicked tongue are all the better to eat you with. Now take off those pants or I'll tear them off."

Ten seconds later, her bottom half was completely bared to him.

"Drop your knees open. Show me all of you."

Her hesitation vanished.

"My, what a pretty pussy you have." Wyn lowered his head and lapped at the sticky, sweet goodness at the entrance to her body. "I want to fuck you with my mouth, Melissa."

"Yes."

He saw no need to hurry. He explored, mapping her folds with his tongue. He licked fast, then slow. He suckled her pussy lips together, then separately. He grazed her clit with his teeth. By the time he knew the taste of her and the shape of her beneath his mouth, he also knew what maneuver his tongue could do to get her to buck her hips up. Now it was time to know what she sounded like when she came against his face, just how hard she could pull his hair, and how many times he could make her come before she begged him to stop.

Ten minutes later, he had the answers to those questions, and more.

Melissa made a timeout sign.

Wyn chuckled against the top of her thigh.

"You are a menace with that mouth," she panted.

"Come on, Amazing Slut-Girl, you can take some more."

She shook her head. "Not with that lizard-like tongue, Super Man-Slut. But that cock of yours?" She smirked, fished a condom out of her cleavage and flicked it at him. "Bring it on home, baby."

He'd never gotten undressed that fast. He was suited up, on her, and in her. She was hot, slick, tight, and perfect. As he rocked into her, she licked and nipped at his lips, searching his mouth for a taste of herself, which was so fucking sexy, he couldn't stand it.

Then her hands were in his hair, clutching his ass, reaching between them to cup his balls—Christ that felt good.

Melissa arched her back and moaned, "Harder. As hard as you can. I'm close again."

A dozen more deep strokes that sent her sliding across the carpet and she came undone.

Her moment of bliss was a beautiful thing to watch.

When that moment came for him, the last thing he saw before he closed his eyes was the same greedy look on her face that he knew had been on his when she'd unraveled.

After he was spent, he buried his face in her neck. And blew a raspberry until she shrieked and pushed him away.

She'd left the light on for him, jumped onboard for hot, welcome home sex right on the damn carpet, and she'd cooked for him.

This cohabitating thing might be better than he thought.

Chapter Six

After they finished eating, Wyn said, "Level with me. You haven't been competing this year."

Melissa wiped her mouth and set her napkin on the table. "Not since March. Partially because I burned out on it. Partially because London wasn't on the circuit anymore. Partially because I realized my life hadn't changed in the past seven years. I decided to take a break."

"That's understandable. But why did you hedge when I asked you about it?"

She shrugged. "It's gotten to be a habit. I'm really glad for the chance to try something different."

"And I can't wait to show my appreciation for all your hard work." He waggled his eyebrows.

"So can you give me an idea on what to expect, rancher man?"

"We've left the cattle in the summer grazing areas as long as possible. Starting the day after tomorrow, we'll move them into pastures closer to home. That's always traumatic for the cattle, so they'll need five days to get back up to a saleable weight. Then we'll start separating and loading them. We have different places that take them, and they have set times when they'll accept shipments, so the shipping process seems endless."

"So we'll all be on horseback?"

"For the cattle drive, we'll take the horse trailer and horses to the edge of the summer grazing area. We'll unload the horses and start driving cattle out of there. One thing that sucks is we'll have to cross two roads, but they're not paved roads and we've never had a run-in with a car. Then after the cattle are settled, we'll come back, ditch the horses, and two of us will drive out to retrieve the horse trailer. Usually Dad is the one who does that."

He also drives ahead and opens the gate so we don't have to stop the cattle and make them wait. But we'll have to figure something else out since we're shorthanded—even with our hot, new cutting horse expert helping out."

Melissa smiled at him. "Flattery will not get me up at the butt crack of dawn to open gates for you, cowboy."

"Maybe I'll make so much noise in the bedroom that you'll have no choice but to get up."

"I have zero problem locking my door at night to ensure that doesn't happen."

Wyn frowned. "You locking me out of my own bedroom?"

"No, because I won't be sleeping in your room, Wynton."

"Explain that."

"I'm set up in the guest bedroom. I have no problem fucking when and where the mood strikes us, but when it's time to sleep...to be blunt, I want my own space. You've lived alone long enough that you'll probably need your own space too—you just don't know it yet. I'll be here three weeks. I don't want to wear out my welcome on the third day because I've strewn my girl stuff all over your bedroom and bathroom. And some nights I can't sleep, so I'm up late reading."

She had an excuse to cover all the bases. He couldn't argue with them, but that didn't mean he wouldn't try like hell to change her mind. He pushed his empty plate back. "So what are we doin' the rest of the night?"

"Dishes first." She kissed his nose. "Ain't domestic life bliss?"

* * * *

The next morning, Wyn hauled his ass out of bed at first light. He and Cres did chores without saying much besides mumbling every once in a while. They stopped by their folks' place to see how Dad was faring. He was tired—and annoyed by the "no ranch work" edict—so for the first time in years, they talked about other things over lunch. Wyn didn't leave in a rush because he was dodging his mom's questions about his relationship with Melissa, he was just anxious to hang out with her the rest of the day.

Once he got back to his house, he felt stupid, coming home early, expecting she'd drop everything and want to spend time with him. She was here as a favor to them to do ranch work. Since her help wasn't needed yet, he had no right to assume she'd want to spend her free time with him.

She sat cross-legged on his couch with her laptop and looked up, beaming a smile at him. "Hey. You done already?"

"For now. Why?"

"Because I want you to take me for a joy ride across the ranch in your truck, cowboy."

His heart simultaneously stopped and exploded with hope. "For real?"

"Unless you want to ride horses to show me the sights?"

"Nope. Let's go." Wyn would drag this afternoon out. Show her every nook and cranny, every field and stream, every rocky ridge and meadow of this place he loved.

Melissa proved to be an excellent gate opener, and she was properly awed by the ranch. That earned her brownie points when he parked in his favorite secluded spot and undressed her.

The times they'd been intimate had been fast and intense. For this go around, Wyn wanted slow. Maybe a little sweet.

His new roomie proved herself to be excellent at slow and sweet, with lazy kisses and lingering caresses.

Afterward, when they were both sweaty and spent on the seat of his truck, he kissed her chest as they spiraled down from the orgasmic high together.

"We're going to wear each other out," she murmured in his hair.

Wyn didn't see a problem with that. "Is that a challenge?"

She groaned. "Not today. I wouldn't mind going back. I need to make a phone call and then I want to exercise Plato."

"Okay. But, baby you gotta move off my lap and let go of my hair so I can drive."

"Oh. Right."

He loved that dazed look in her eyes, knowing he'd put it there.

* * * *

Two nights later, after another nutritious—and surprisingly delicious meal—Wyn broke out the PlayStation 4 and they played Borderlands.

"I'm surprised you're a gamer," he said.

"There's not a lot of other things to do on the road once I get the rig parked for the night."

Wyn smirked at her. "You ain't out rounding up a one-night rodeo for yourself every night? For shame, Amazing Slut-Girl. I'm disappointed."

"My cooter is way more selective these days." She shifted on the couch. "And dude, I've never had this much sex, consistently with the same guy. My cooter is clapping with joy, at the same time she's like…you expect me to take the ground and pound twice daily *and* get chafed in the saddle all day? Pass the ice pack, please."

He laughed. Christ. She made him laugh like no other woman he'd ever met. And laughing with her so much felt damn good. "You sayin' you want me to dial it back?"

"No fucking way, Super Man-Slut. My cooter does not speak for me."

Really, really crazy about this woman already.

"So what else did you do to kill time?" Onscreen he dodged a flurry of arrows and slid beneath a boulder.

"I listen to audiobooks when I'm driving. When I'm at an event, I'm out among the contestants and rodeo people because I spend enough time by myself getting to the destination."

"Do you have an apartment that's a home base?"

Onscreen, Melissa chopped a monster's head off with a broadsword, then snagged the jeweled necklace off the corpse with a, "I'll take that, sucker," before she answered. "I had a place in Kentucky. Once I stopped going there…I put my money into the nicest horse trailer I could buy. I have everything I need. I've upgraded it twice. But since I've been working at Grade A, I rented a place in town to see if I liked living in one place again."

"What's the verdict?"

She shrugged. "Still out. At least for there. Why?"

Wyn maneuvered around a patch of quicksand onscreen. "Sutton made great money when he was winning. Bulldogging paid for his house, and he's never been short on cash for anything else. But I heard other guys talkin' like they don't make a living at it."

"You asking how I support myself because you're looking for me to pay you rent while I'm here?"

"No, smartass." He bristled. "Forget it."

Melissa hit pause on the game and faced him. "Let's get this out in the open. I have Kentucky blueblood parents, remember? I have a trust fund. I use it when I need to. I'm not one of those 'Oh, I have to make it on my own even if I have to live in a hovel to prove I'm independent' kind of women. My grandparents set the trust fund up for me at birth. I was a one hundred percent scholarship recipient for college, so I didn't touch my college fund. I made enough money competing to support myself, but I'm lucky enough to have a financial cushion that allows me to not worry that I'll have to eat Ramen noodles for a month so I can afford to fill my truck up with gas to get to the next event."

"You don't have to get defensive."

"I'm not. This is just another example of why I don't tell anyone my background."

He twined a long, red curl around his index finger. "Doesn't that get lonely? Not letting anyone see the real you?"

She laughed harshly. "Being on the road and competing is the *real* me. The girl I was before? She's long gone." She tried to get away from him and succeeded, despite that he'd nearly pulled her hair out in the process.

"Come back here."

"Why?"

"So you can look into my eyes when I tell you this." He stroked her jawline with his thumb. "I like the real you. A lot. And not just because you're the sexiest woman I've ever been with, or that you have a lewd sense of humor, or that you like to fuck as much as I do."

She raised a dark red eyebrow. "You *are* going somewhere with this, right cowboy?"

"Yep. You're the first woman I've invited to stay at my place for longer than a few hours. You're the first woman who's played video games with me. You're not the first woman to cook for me, but you didn't create that meal like it was a wife audition."

"Dude, if I was auditioning to be your wife, I'd cook naked."

Wyn smiled. "See? You're so goddamned funny. I just wanna sit here and talk to you for hours. And this is all new to me, okay? And yet, it's so damn easy. You just slipped in here like you belong. But without permanent ties to anything, I worry that you'll slip back out just as easily." Jesus. Did that make him sound whiny?

Melissa stared at him. "I don't know where this will go, Wynton. I feel like I've known you for years when it's just been days. But I can't promise you anything when I'm taking things—my life—day by day."

Not what he wanted to hear, but it'd have to do for now. "Fair enough." He kissed her forehead. "Let's get back to the game. I believe you were about to pillage the village."

* * * *

For the next week, much to Wyn's annoyance, Melissa had stuck to her guns and locked the door to the guest bedroom after she went to bed. Alone. Every night. It was still locked in the morning—and his need to check that every morning just pissed him off. So prior to them saying good night, he felt entitled to poke her—promising he'd never lock her out of his room and he'd welcome any late visits from her.

He banked his disappointment that she hadn't taken him up on his offer even one time in the last seven nights.

So when a warm body crawled in bed beside him, he figured he was dreaming.

Soft hands floated over his arms and across his shoulders. Cool lips landed on the back of his neck, sending a shudder through him.

"Wynton? Are you awake?"

He groaned. "I am now. What time is it?"

"Three."

Christ. "You know what time we have to get up to start loading cattle?"

"Yes."

"Then what are you doin' in my bed, Miss I-Lock-My-Doors? Did you have a bad dream or something?"

"No. I had a good dream." She licked the vertebra at the base of his skull. "A sexy dream." She blew a stream of air across the damp spot she'd created. "A dirty dream. Starring dirty-minded, hot-bodied you." She sank her teeth into the nape of his neck.

It was as if that particular spot had a direct line to his cock, and it immediately went rock-fucking-hard.

She whispered, "I came in here to see if you wanted me to act out the good parts of my dream."

"Fuck, yeah."

Melissa rolled him to his back. "It's handy that you sleep naked, cowboy."

He kept his room so dark he could only make out her shape in the greenish glow from the digital clock on the side of the bed. "So you're waking me up to reward me with sex?"

"Are you sure you're awake? Or is this a dream starring the sleep sex fairy?" She slid down his body and beneath the covers.

Then her warm, wet mouth engulfed his cock. He clenched his hands and his ass cheeks to keep from bowing up.

By the time she quit teasing—deep-throating him, licking just the head of his cock with the tip of her tongue while she jacked him—his entire body vibrated.

She rolled a condom down his shaft and straddled him, burying his length inside her hot and slick cunt an inch at a time.

"Melissa."

She stretched her body across his and put her mouth on his ear. "I want to fuck you slowly and send you soaring without all the thrusting and straining, so when you do tip over the edge into the abyss, you'll wonder if it all had been a dream."

Wyn sank into the pillows and let her have her way with him, as she sucked and nibbled on his neck, his ears, and his chest. She rocked his cock in and out in the dreamy rhythm she'd mentioned. He trailed his fingertips up and down her spine, pleased to feel gooseflesh erupting in their wake.

When his balls drew up and he felt that tingle at the base of his spine, he grabbed onto her ass and let her body pull the orgasm from his.

She feathered kisses over his lips and disconnected their bodies. She even removed the condom. After one last kiss she said, "Reality is always much sweeter than dreams," and slipped from his room.

The next morning he might've believed it *had* all been a dream…but the hickey above his left nipple was proof she'd been there.

Maybe she was coming around. Maybe next time she'd be in his bed all night.

Chapter Seven

Over the past two weeks, Mel had become a decent ranch hand. After spending long days in the saddle and long nights christening every surface in Wynton's house, she was dragging serious ass today. Ranch work wasn't for wimps.

Luckily, her years of cutting competition had proved useful when keeping stray heifers in line. Seemed those stubborn cows always made a beeline for the creek. She could understand it if it was hot, but the weather had cooled off considerably, and it was always colder down by the water.

She shivered in her borrowed Carhartt coat. She couldn't believe how fast the time had gone. It seemed like yesterday that she'd unpacked her things, half-worried/half-excited to share living space with Wynton. She'd learned so much about him—not just his sexual preferences.

Now she knew little...domestic things. He brewed his first two cups of coffee in the morning as thick as tar. He ate lunch with his parents and brother most days. He read the newspaper from front to back before supper. He liked the scent of laundry detergent in the air so he did one load of clothes every day. He preferred sitcoms to dramas on TV. He shaved every day—not just because she was there.

Now that she also knew the core of him—his fierce love of his life as a rancher and being around his family, his connection to his animals and the land—she realized she'd never find another man like him. She hated that their time together was coming to a close. Wynton had been vague when she'd asked about his plans after the shipping was done, so she hadn't brought it up again.

Plato did a little crow-hop and she absentmindedly reached down and patted his neck. "Easy. I know you wanna work, but we gotta let the boys do their stuff."

Boys. That was almost a derogatory term for the masculine perfection of Wynton and Creston Grant. Seeing them work together was like watching a ballet. Each move and counter move perfectly choreographed. Ropes thrown in unison or in opposition. Both of them taking off on their horses at the same speed. Wynton cut left, while Cres cut right, and the herd was immediately back on track, going where the Grant boys wanted them to go.

She looked around at the pine trees lining this valley that dipped below the rock outcroppings. Some of the grass still had the barest hint of green, but even the brown stalks added to the visual appeal of vastness and serenity. She truly loved it here. It was so peaceful.

When her fingertips tingled and she knew it wasn't from cold, she dug into her pocket and took out a box of raisins. The first few days she hadn't done much strenuous activity—unless lots of hot sex, a couple times a day counted—and she had good blood sugar numbers. She felt great. Better than she had since before the diagnosis. She felt…normal. When her daily activity kicked up the past two weeks, she'd adjusted quickly and had no adverse effects. So she was beginning to think that finally after six and a half months, she had a handle on living with diabetes.

And since things were going better between her and Wynton than she ever imagined, she hadn't seen a need to test their relationship to see if telling him about her condition changed things. A smarmy voice in her head said, *Great plan, Mel. Tell him about it the first time he acts like a total jackass.*

Wynton whistled, drawing her attention to the loading chutes.

Damn, damn, damn but that man was fine. Hard-working, determined, thoughtful, funny, interesting. What you saw with him was exactly what you got. And in her eyes that made him damn near perfect.

You have fallen for him.

Who wouldn't?

She let her gaze scan the panoramic view. She could get used to this life. Working side by side—or at least in close proximity to her man. Raising cattle and maybe a few kids.

Whoa.

Whoa, whoa, whoa.

Putting the cart before the horse, much? Get through the next week with him before you start picking out baby names and knitting fucking booties.

"Melissa!"

Her head snapped up.

All Wynton had to do was point and she knew where she was supposed to be. Her gaze zeroed in on the problem cow. She clicked at Plato.

But before they reached the edge of the herd, the cow headed for the stock tank. On the other side of the pasture.

Then they were off on a wild cow chase.

Plato's withers quivered with excitement. He was in his glory as a cow horse. By the third day, he was penned with Charlie, Wyn's horse, Petey, Cres's horse, and Ringo, Jim's horse. By the fourth day in the field with the Grant horses, Plato had taken over as the leader.

The cow was fast. But Plato was faster.

Mel cut around and Plato's back end slid out so they were almost parallel to the ground. But Plato righted himself and they were in front of the cow, Plato moving back and forth as he tried to gauge which way the cow intended to bolt.

The cow heard the herd mooing behind her. Seeing no escape, she slowly turned around and lumbered back to the corral.

Plato kept on her until she was back where she belonged.

Something was spooking the herd today. Mel had to chase over a dozen runaways. So it took twice as long to sort and load. She'd depleted her secret store of snacks in her pockets and her water bottle was empty.

Wynton wasn't on horseback today. He slammed the back end of the livestock hauler and then jogged up to the driver's side to talk to Cres, who was delivering the cattle.

Mel dismounted. The cold seemed to have settled in her bones, so she led Plato into the barn to warm up as she removed the tack and brushed him down. She had to give him his special blend of oats out of the view of the other horses so they wouldn't fight for their share.

She'd just sent him out into the corral and locked the gate, when a wave of dizziness overtook her. She patted her hand along the fence, trying to squint through the white spots dancing in front of her eyes for the outside pump. There. Red handle. Once she reached it, she pulled up the handle. She had to hold on to the metal pipe as she held one shaking hand out to the stream of water. Very little liquid was flowing into the plastic; it was just getting her hand wet.

Fuck it.

Mel bent down and gulped water directly from the gushing stream. Water had pooled in the rocks, but she didn't care. She was so damn thirsty.

When she'd had enough, she yanked the handle down and cut off the flow. She pushed herself upright and wiped her face on the sleeve of her coat.

Of course that's when she noticed Wyn standing in the doorway of the barn.

He raised both eyebrows. "Thirsty?"

"Very."

"You hydrated now?"

Mel watched him stalk closer with that look in his eyes. A look that said he was about to strip her down and rock her body to the core. "Yes I am."

"Good."

"So, what's going on?"

"You."

"What about me?"

"You are driving me absolutely fucking crazy."

She waited.

"Do you have any idea how sexy you are on a horse? So regal? So intuitive? Fuck, I love to watch you make lightning quick adjustments when you're on the outside of the herd." He moved closer. "I'm surprised I can get any work done at all because I can't take my eyes off of you. For the past two weeks I've watched you. Watched that crazy red hair tossed by the wind as you're chasin' down strays. Watched your cheeks turn pink with color. Watched your eyes dancing with excitement and concentration. You're beautiful, Melissa. But when you're so focused on your task, doin' what you're so goddamned good at, you take my fucking breath away."

Her heart raced. Even when she'd just gulped water, her mouth had gone dry. While he was getting closer, she'd started backing up in a circle, retreating into the barn.

"And every day, when my cock is so fucking hard I could pound horseshoes with it, I tell myself to wait until I can take you in my bed, or on my couch, or on the damn washing machine. But today, Cres is gone, and it's just you and me. Today, I ain't gonna wait."

His eyes were hot and dark and focused one hundred percent on her.

"No foreplay. No sweet kisses or tender touches. I want you, hard and fast and rough. I wanna bend you over and fuck you until the ache of wantin' you doesn't consume me like this."

Two more steps back. "Wynton."

"You want this. I can see it in your eyes. I bet your nipples are hard. I bet your pussy is already wet."

"So?"

"So, stop movin' so we can get on with it."

"Or what?"

"There is no *or*. Don't make me chase you down."

"Think you can catch me, cowboy?" God. Why was she taunting him?

His deep, rasping, sarcastic laugh might've been the sexiest thing she'd ever heard. "Oh, yeah? How about I'll even give you a head start. I'll count to five."

Mel turned and ran.

From behind she heard, "Onetwothreefourfive."

She managed to get out, "That's cheating!" before an arm banded around her waist and she was airborne. She shrieked.

"That's it, baby," he growled in her ear. "Get those vocal cords warmed up because before I'm done with you, you're gonna be screaming my name."

Wynton carried her—one-armed no less!—into the tack room. He pulled a saddle blanket out of the stack and draped it over a workbench. Then he set her on her feet and stripped off her coat. His voice was back in her ear. "Chest on the bench, ass in the air is how I want you. Hold on to the bench with your left hand and drop your right hand beside your leg."

Her need for him overtook any thoughts of arguing. Wynton had been the most spectacular lover she'd ever had, but he'd never been like…this. Desperate to have her and sort of pissed off about it.

At first he didn't touch her besides undoing her jeans, shoving them and her underwear to the tops of her boots, then kicking her feet out to widen her stance.

She heard his labored breaths as he shed his clothing. She heard the crinkle of a condom wrapper. She felt his satisfied grunt on the back of her neck when he pressed his chest to her back and reached between her legs to find her dripping wet.

One finger entered her. Then two. God. He had such long, thick fingers. She made a soft gasp when the callused pad of his thumb connected with her clit.

Wynton kept her immobilized on the bench, his breath hot in her ear as he finger fucked her. And he knew just where to stroke inside her pussy walls and for how long. He knew how much direct contact her clit could take. He knew how to light the fuse and how long before she detonated.

"It's mine, Melissa. Give it to me."

She did cry out when the orgasm blasted through her.

He kept pumping and doing that flicking thing on her clit, dragging out her pleasure. When the last pulse ended, he stilled and pulled his fingers out of her. Then he whispered, "Don't. Move."

No problem. She was pretty sure her spine was somewhere on the hay-strewn floor below her.

He slapped his hands on her ass cheeks hard enough to make that one swat sting. His two fingers, wet with her juices, trailed down her butt crack to her anus. He swept his fingers across her hole until the nerve endings flared to life and the rim was sticky.

She stilled. They'd talked about anal sex, even done a little anal play back and forth, and she knew he wanted to shove his cock in her ass. She wanted that too, but she needed to be more prepared than just a couple of swipes of her come to ease the way.

Wynton's tight grip on her ass relaxed. She felt the damp heat of his breath on her lower back right before he kissed the spot and started to drag his tongue down the split in her ass, making a soft growling noise as he followed the trail he'd made with her juices. And when he reached her anus, he licked and lapped and sucked that tight ring before he plunged his tongue inside.

"Oh, God." He did it a few more times, driving her crazy with the raunchy sensation that she loved.

Then he tilted her hips and inserted just the tip of his cock into her pussy. He dangled something rough against her right leg that caused her to twitch before he slid it into her hand. She squeezed her fingers around it. It felt like...rope.

Holy fuck.

Still breathing heavily, still just resting his cock an inch inside her, Wynton guided her hand between her thighs.

Keeping his hand circling her wrist, he dragged the rope across her clit.

Mel arched up. She tried to pull her hand away, but Wynton wouldn't allow it.

"Ride that line between pleasure and pain."

"I-I...what if it's too much?"

Once again he layered his chest to her back. "There's no such thing." He sucked on her earlobe, impaled her fully, and pulled the rope across her clit all at the same time.

She screamed.

Wynton fucked her as rough and fast and hard as he'd warned he would. His harsh grunts, the sucking sounds of her pussy with his every stroke, the *thump thump thump* of the bench legs echoed around her.

Even before she started to come, Mel drifted to that place where anticipation met intent. She furiously rubbed her clit, her stomach tight every time the twine scraped over that swollen nub. But she couldn't stop. It was so close... It was right...there.

The orgasm ripped through her. Her clit throbbed like she'd never felt it. Her pussy clamped down so hard on Wynton's cock that she swore she could feel his heart pounding as he plowed into her. Every part of her body tingled. Her ears rang, her head went muzzy. She sucked in a deep breath and the last thing she heard before she passed out was Wynton roaring like a beast.

* * * *

She'd blacked out.

Now Wynton had to know something was wrong with her. Women didn't just pass the fuck out during sex—even as mind-blowing as that sex had been. At least she hadn't checked out before the orgasm that would forevermore be "the orgasm" that all others would be judged by.

She wiggled her naked body. She turned her head. The pillow smelled like him. The scent immediately soothed her. As did the rough-skinned palm that skated down her arm.

"Hey, sleepyhead."

"Uh, how'd I get here?"

"You were seriously out of it after we...you know."

The man was embarrassed? Get out.

"So I carried you into the house, undressed you, and tucked you in my bed."

"How long have I been here?"

"Half an hour." A soft kiss landed on her shoulder. "I fucked you so hard that you passed out, baby." Another kiss. "I've never had that happen before."

Now he sounded so smug. "It's never happened to me before either."

"One for the record books, Amazing Slut-Girl."

Mel smiled in the dark. "True dat, Super Man-Slut." The more conscious she became, the less it felt like she'd had an...episode. Maybe she was just thirsty, hungry, and tired because she'd worked all day, followed by getting spun inside out and upside down by one of the most intense sexual encounters of her life. What woman wouldn't pass out from being exposed to Wynton Grant's pheromones and sating his beastly sexual appetite after he'd made her come so hard she'd screamed? Twice?

"You all right?" he murmured.

"Mmm-hmm. I need to eat something and I'm really thirsty. But besides that..." She stretched. "I feel thoroughly fucked."

He chuckled. "Me too. You sore?"

"A little."

"My fault. Lemme fix that." He slipped beneath the covers and positioned himself between her legs. He planted the softest kisses on her abraded clit.

"Wynton—"

"I just fucked you hard, fast, and rough, Melissa. Now let me make love to you slow and sweet."

Like she could say no to that.

Chapter Eight

In the last three weeks, Wyn's life had changed completely.

He'd fallen in love.

With a hookup.

A *wedding* hookup, no less.

It's been more than a hookup since the first time you kissed her, dumbass.

True.

Wyn was done denying this was a *one and done* or *hit it and quit it* scenario. Melissa was meant to be his. Not for just a few lousy weeks, either. Now he just hoped that Melissa could see he was "the one" she'd been looking for.

How had he gotten so lucky? She was everything he'd wanted and feared he'd never find. She was perfect.

Perfect.

She'd proven it so many times, in so many ways.

She could ride a horse like no woman he'd ever seen.

She liked to just sit around and bullshit.

She liked to play video games.

She liked to play darts and pool.

She liked to curl up on the couch and watch TV.

She liked to cook.

She had a great sense of humor.

She loved sex—anytime, anyplace. She was as inventive in her suggestions as she was adventurous with his.

With each new thing he discovered about her, he fell harder for her.

Why was he reminding himself of all these awesome things about her?

Because Melissa had been a little...grouchy since yesterday. It wasn't his fault that she'd fallen asleep in his bed after he'd made love to her. When she woke up—cranky as hell—she stormed off to her bed, insisting she slept better alone.

How would she know that if she hadn't actually tried sleeping in his bed an entire night?

Maybe he'd man up and ask her that when he got home. He grinned. That'd get her riled up—and that was how he loved her best.

He slowed down and pulled into Cres's driveway.

Cres was out of his house as soon as Wyn killed the ignition. As Wyn wandered up the driveway with a six-pack of Fat Tire beer, Cres said, "That's your *we've gotta talk* look. So it's finally time to deal with Dad's bombshell?"

"I didn't want this to be a pressure thing, Cres. I guess we could've discussed this while we were movin' cattle."

Cres dropped the tailgate on his truck. "Mel's been around and it didn't seem right to talk in circles or exclude her from our conversation. And every other time we've been together it's been with Dad and Mom."

Wyn hopped onto the tailgate beside his brother and handed him a beer.

"Thanks." Cres said, "Does it surprise you that Dad hasn't been bugging us to make a decision?"

"Dad's got other things on his mind for a change. I'm happy to see that. Mom is too. So to be honest, I don't think they care one way or another what our decision is because they've already made theirs. Make sense?"

"Yeah. And Mom's too busy harassing you about what's going on with you and Mel." Cres sipped his beer. "Speaking of Mel...you two seem very happy to be playing house."

Wyn scowled. "I *hate* that fucking term."

"What else can you call it if it's not a trial run for the real deal?"

"Piss off. And her name is Melissa, not Mel. Mel...well, that's more in line with your tastes."

Cres laughed. "True. I like her. She's good for you."

"So if I wanted to play house with her for real?"

"I'd probably come over more often since she's a better cook than you."

"Again, Cres, piss off." Wyn cracked his beer. "I want her there for the long haul. Not just because she's a good cook but because she's...everything. I just feel in my gut she's it for me."

"Does she feel that way too?"

"I hope so."

"Man, Sutton is *so* gonna rub it in your face that you're pussy-whipped."

"I deserve it." He grinned. "I *welcome* it. Anyway, you've had a couple of weeks to think about Dad's offer. Made any decisions yet?"

Cres looked at him oddly. "It never really was a decision for me, bro. I like ranching with you. It'd suck to do it by myself. I say let's keep it together. Same as it's always been."

Wyn held his bottle to his brother's for a toast. "Amen."

A few moments of silence passed.

"Since it seemed like *you* were dragging this decision out, I thought maybe you were gonna suggest we divvy it up."

Wyn pinned him with a sharp look. "Why in the hell would you say that?"

Cres shrugged. "I came out last year. Everyone in the family has been supportive—even more than I expected. But supporting me in my personal life and bein' offered a chance to cut ties with me professionally because of *how* I live my life… We both know it might affect who wants to do business with both of us, Wyn. I could see that dividing it would be an easy out for everyone. I think that's why Dad offered it as a suggestion."

"Bullshit. I thought *you* might be lookin' for an out from ranching completely," Wyn said. "Trying to figure out a way to sell your portion to me."

"And what would I do if I wasn't ranching? I've got no interest in doin' anything else, so selling never even crossed my mind," Cres said. "Besides, knowing us, even if we divided it up, we'd still work together most days anyway."

"True." Wyn swallowed a mouthful of beer. "So we good?"

"I reckon. Be weird not havin' Dad around day-to-day. I'm gonna miss him and those fucked up curse word combinations he uses when he's frustrated."

Wyn smiled. "I'm gonna miss him too. He and Mom deserve a chance to spend the money he's been saving all these years. As for us…dividing the profits by two instead of by three will take some getting used to."

Cres grinned. "That extra cash will come in handy for you since you're playin' house."

"Asshole. What about you and Mick? Any thoughts of playin' house with him?"

"It's casual," was all Cres said. "He's comin' to help load for the Denver trip tomorrow."

"That's an overnight trip."

"Yep. If you gotta problem with that, let me know."

Wyn shot him a *don't be an idiot* look. "I don't."

"Good." Cres exhaled. "Thanks. Christ. I don't know fuck-all about havin' a boyfriend, bro."

"Mick keeps comin' back around, so you must know how to do something right." As soon as that left Wyn's mouth, he groaned. "Shit. I didn't mean it that way."

Cres laughed. "How 'bout we don't go there. *Ever*."

"Deal." He smirked. "Although…Melissa said you and Mick together…that'd be live porn she'd watch."

"Jesus. No wonder you love her. She's as perverted as you."

* * * *

After almost three weeks of ranch life, Mel hadn't gotten used to waking up at the butt crack of dawn and hauling her carcass out of a toasty bed.

So Wynton's way-too-early, and way-too-chipper summons, "Up and at 'em, Kentucky," as he beat on her door annoyed the crap out of her.

Mel forced herself to respond, "I'll be there in five," somewhat politely, instead of yelling at him to get the fucking battering ram away from her door.

Yeah. She was punchy and cranky.

After taking her shot of insulin, she shoved a glucose pill in her jeans, packed her coat pockets with snacks and filled her water bottle. The last day of shipping cattle meant everyone was in a hurry, so she didn't have time for coffee or breakfast.

Mistake number one.

Once she'd saddled up and the sun had come out, she'd immediately overheated. She took her jacket off and tossed it over a fencepost.

Mistake number two.

Since this was the largest group of cattle going to market, of course everything went wrong. Which meant she spent four hours chasing down runaways and culling cows from the milling herd.

Four hours without a break, without water, and without her trusty snacks.

Mistake number three.

But rather than tell Wynton she hit the hypoglycemic stage and was about to crash, she decided it'd be better to just go off and crash alone.

Mistake number four.

The edges of her conscious began to shrink in on her like a camera viewfinder that starts out close, but objects get smaller and farther away until everything is fuzzy and ringed with black.

She rode to the barn and dismounted. If she could just have a few minutes of clarity to unsaddle her horse while those guys—loaded or unloaded the cattle?—she couldn't remember, she could probably make it to the house before she collapsed.

Wait. The house was collapsing? Why?

She was so confused.

Where was she? What happened to her horse?

Mel spun around and that action caused a quick spike of pain. She tried to pat the top of her head to see if some asshole had buried an ax in her skull, but she ended up smacking herself in the face.

Fuck that hurt.

Take a pill for it.

Good plan. She dug in her pocket—why weren't her fingers working?—and found a round, white thing. She squinted at it. After enclosing it in her fist, she went to find water. She took two steps forward and swayed.

Whoa. When had she gotten on the carousel? Why was everything spinning so fast it was blurred? What was that loud, whooshing noise?

She made it to a bale of straw before the darkness overcame her.

Chapter Nine

After the cattle truck rumbled down the driveway, Wyn did loading chute maintenance—his least favorite part of shipping cattle. But if he didn't fix the problems now, they'd have issues the next time they used the chutes because he wouldn't remember what needed done.

He'd welcomed Mick's help today. Wyn was especially grateful that Mick was riding with Cres to the sale barn, so Wyn could catch up on the piles of paperwork that always accompanied selling cattle. Cres and Mick planned to stay overnight in Denver before heading home. He wouldn't begrudge his brother a little personal time since he'd come to realize how much he needed that in his own life.

Speaking of...he wondered where his hot, redheaded cattle cutting expert had gone. She'd been acting a little weird toward the end.

He saw Plato in the corral, but it looked like he still wore a bridle and bit. Melissa would never turn him out like that.

"Melissa?"

No response.

An eerie feeling rippled down his spine. "Melissa?" he called into the barn.

No answer.

If his head had been turned the other direction, he might've missed her. But the red in her corduroy shirt snagged his attention. He sauntered up to the hay bale she sat on and noticed her eyes were closed. "Napping on the job, Kentucky? For shame."

Melissa didn't acknowledge him at all.

Man, she was really asleep. But as soon as he stood in front of her, he knew she wasn't napping. Something was wrong with her.

He crouched down and took her hand. Holy shit, it was like ice. But he saw her forehead was damp with perspiration and her face was flushed. He tried to shake her. "Melissa?"

She mumbled something.

"Baby, you're scarin' me." Wyn noticed her other hand was closed in a tight fist. He pried her fingers open and saw she'd clutched a white pill. He remembered her complaining of a bad headache last night before she'd gone to bed in her own room. How many of these had she taken?

When her body started to shake uncontrollably and even that didn't wake her up, he dug his cell phone out of his pocket and dialed 911.

After he'd given them the information, hearing the word overdose—which he vehemently argued against, he decided to buck the operator's judgment and move Melissa to the ground.

He'd just propped her head on his jacket when he heard the unmistakable sound of a cattle truck rumbling up the driveway.

His annoyance that Cres had forgotten something *again*, was immediately replaced with a sense of urgency. Mick had medical training.

Wyn carefully lifted Melissa into his arms and carried her out of the barn. He'd made it halfway to the house when both men jumped out of the cab of the truck and ran toward him.

"What happened?" Cres demanded.

"I don't know. I found her like this. Mick, help her," he pleaded.

"Completely unresponsive?"

"Yes. Then she started to shake, almost like she was having a seizure."

"Take her in the house. You called 911?"

"Just got off the phone with them, but they said it'll be at least fifteen minutes."

Once they were inside, Wyn laid Melissa on the couch. He hovered over her as Mick poked and prodded her.

"Is she on any medication?"

"I don't know." He paused. "Wait, she had this in her hand." He passed over the pill.

Mick held it up to the light and frowned.

"What?"

"It's a glucose pill."

"What's that?"

"Diabetics take them when their blood sugar levels are low." Mick looked up at him. "Wyn, is Melissa diabetic?"

"I have no idea. She's never mentioned it to me."

"You haven't seen her testing her blood sugar levels first thing in the morning? Or the last thing before she crawls in bed at night?"

Suddenly, her secretiveness, her insistence on sleeping in her own bed at night and even locking her damn door in the morning made sense. Wyn said, "Fuck. We don't sleep in the same bed. She claimed she's a restless sleeper and needs her own space, so she's been sleeping in the guest bedroom. But obviously it was so she could keep this from me. Why would she do that?"

"Worry about that later. Right now, go into her room and see if you can find a blood glucose meter, some kind of insulin injection instruments. Hopefully she's got a Glucagon rescue kit."

Wyn looked at Cres with utter confusion. "What did he say?"

"Mick, under the circumstances it'd be better for you to do it since you know what to look for," Cres said.

"Where's her room?"

"Last one at the end of the hallway."

Mick took off.

Wyn dropped to his knees beside Melissa. He picked up her hand and kissed her knuckles. "You and me are gonna have a serious talk when you're not goddamned unconscious."

"Promise me you won't yell at her for this when she comes around."

He turned and glared at Cres. "Why the fuck would you even say that to me?"

"For that reason right there. You get angry first and maybe you'll try reasonable later. I'm askin' you not to do that this time. There's a reason she kept this from you. If you want to understand why, don't scare her off with your blustering and accusations." He softened his tone. "I know you care about her. And I know she's crazy about you. So don't wreck this. Just...tread lightly okay?"

Mick jogged back into the room. He held up a kit. "She's got one."

"You know what to do?"

"Yeah. You gotta move, man," Mick said to him. "Oh, and I found her medic alert bracelet. She is diabetic. Type 1. She's insulin dependent."

Wyn was absolutely poleaxed. This woman that he'd bared his soul to, opened his home to, made love to and had fallen for...hadn't trusted him enough to share this with him.

"This will help her out a lot," Mick said.

"Should I call and cancel the ambulance?" Wyn asked.

"No. The paramedics will need to assess her. They might even take her to the hospital since it sounds like she might've had a seizure."

Seizure. That word twisted his guts into a knot. He couldn't watch as Mick...did whatever he did, because Wyn would be tempted to ask a million questions. The time for questions would come later.

Time passed in an endless void as he paced.

Finally, he heard Mick say, "No, Mel, don't try and sit up."

Melissa said something too low for Wyn to hear. But Mick's response was loud and clear. "Yes, he's here."

She was asking for him?

Wyn crossed the room and stood behind Mick. A sick feeling twisted his stomach again. Until he heard her whisper...

"Tell him I love him."

Say what?

"I'm sure he'll appreciate hearing that." Mick sent Wyn an apologetic look. "She's babbling."

But I want her to mean it.

Mick kept up a running dialogue, if only to keep Melissa from talking. "It's only been twenty minutes since we left. We had to turn around because Cres left the paperwork and his wallet in the tack room."

"Wyn?"

What the hell? She never called him Wyn. She always called him by his full name. It appeared she didn't know what she was saying. "Yeah, baby, I'm here."

Melissa's skin was blotchy, red in spots, pasty white in others. Her eyes were vacant. But when she saw him? Her eyes held fear. And then a film of tears. Her lips started to wobble after she mouthed "sorry" and then she turned her head into the couch cushion, away from him.

The fuck that was happening. She was goddamn *done* hiding anything from him. Wyn stepped in front of Mick and braced his hand on the wall above the back of the couch, so he loomed above her. He reached down and gently turned her face toward him. "Kentucky, look at me."

"Wyn," Cres warned.

"Butt out, bro. This is between me and my woman."

That got Melissa's eyes to open again.

He stroked his thumb over her cheek. "There she is, my beautiful, stubborn filly. Fair warning, darlin'. After the EMTs get here and tell me what steps I need to take to get you back to normal, you and me are gonna have a serious talk."

"You're mad at me," she choked out.

"No, I'm scared for you. Big difference. Now I'm gonna let Mick do his thing. I just wanted you to know I'm here and I ain't goin' anywhere."

Her eyes teared up again and she nodded before she closed her eyes.

The paramedics arrived.

Wyn hung on the periphery and tried to decipher what they were saying as they spoke to her and Mick. Even when he knew it was ridiculous, he had a flash of annoyance that the EMTs were talking to Mick about

Melissa's condition when they should've been talking to him. He should know this stuff. Every single bit of it. He vowed he'd never be kept out of the loop again when it came to Melissa's health issues. He'd read everything he could get his hands on so he knew exactly how to help her. And figure out how to prevent this from ever happening again.

The female EMT finally took Wyn aside. "We're not admitting her to the hospital as long as you're comfortable keeping a very close eye on her the next twenty-four hours."

"Absolutely."

"Mick indicated that you weren't aware she was diabetic."

"No, but I can promise you I'll be up to speed on everything about this in the next few hours."

"There's tons of information online—most of it is excellent. Thankfully she had an emergency kit. You'd be surprised how many diabetics aren't so well-prepared. Anyway, she said she took her dose of insulin this morning, so this...episode isn't due to negligence—aka 'forgetting' to inject herself. It sounds like she overexerted herself the past few days."

Wyn experienced a punch of guilt over that. He *had* been working her hard. "The tablet she had in her hand. Is that part of her daily medication?"

"No, it's supposed to be a quick fix when she feels the effects of low blood sugar. That's just one of many choices to get her glycemic index back in balance. She can fill you in on what foods/drinks/snacks usually work best for her when her body tells her she's hypoglycemic."

He should be recording this conversation—all the words were jumbling together.

"As soon as she's feeling up to it, she needs to eat. She'll need to check her blood sugar levels more often. And if rest, liquids, and food don't get her levels back down into the normal range? Bring her to the ER."

"I will."

She patted his shoulder. "I know you will."

Wyn shot a quick glance over his shoulder. "Can I ask...have you seen this before?"

"What? A diabetic starting to go into diabetic shock?"

"No, people close to the patient bein' in the dark about their condition."

She looked thoughtful. "For some people, talking about having diabetes is an embarrassment because of all the misinformation and misperceptions about it, so it's easier to keep it under wraps. I had a friend in high school that went to great lengths to hide it because she didn't want our classmates or teachers to treat her differently or feel sorry for her. Even at age seventeen, she worried that she'd never find love because it would be daunting for a guy to take on a woman with a chronic illness. Maybe that sounds stupid to us, but the truth is, we don't have to be vigilant about food intake, watch physical activity, take insulin shots, do blood sugar monitoring that the people who have this disease have to deal with every day. And like it or not, type 1 diabetes is an incurable disease. That's not to say it's not manageable, but it is a lifelong condition." She paused. "Did that answer your question?"

"Yes. More than you know. Thank you."

By the time the EMTs left, Melissa was sitting up.

Cres and Mick waited in the kitchen. That's where he went first.

"I know you've gotta take off, and this is one time, baby bro, that I won't chew your ass for forgetting paperwork. I'm thankful that you were here, Mick."

"Glad to help. But you need to get to the bottom of why she kept this from you. Show her you're a standup guy, Wyn. Maybe she's never had anyone show her how to stand your ground when the going gets tough."

"I hear ya."

Cres clapped him on the shoulder. "See you tomorrow. You need anything, call or text."

Wyn followed them out and watched the cattle truck drive away for the second time. Then he went back inside to deal with his woman.

Melissa looked so…frail sitting on his couch with an afghan draped over her.

He crouched in front of her. "You feel like eating anything yet?"

"No. The beef jerky and orange juice will hold me over for a bit."

"Good. You ready to get some rest?"

"I thought I'd stretch out on the couch."

He stood. "You thought wrong." He scooped her into his arms. "Hang on."

She didn't speak until she noticed they weren't going in the direction of her room. "Wynton?"

"From here on out, you're sleepin' with me."

"But all my stuff—"

"Will be moved into my room." He set her on the bed and pulled the afghan away. "In my bed is where you should've been all along and you damn well know it."

Melissa didn't argue.

"Now, do you need me to help you take your clothes off? Or do you wanna do it?"

"Stop it," she snapped. "I don't want you to baby me."

Wyn got right in her face. "Tough shit. I want to take care of you and you'll let me, understand? " He exhaled a slow breath. "I need to do this as much as you need to let me do it."

She reached up and touched his face. "Okay. But no funny business when you help me take my clothes off. I don't have the energy for it."

Do not snap at her for believing you're such a sex fiend that you'd take advantage of her after she had a diabetic episode.

"God, I'm sorry for saying that. I was trying to make light of the situation and it didn't come out that way."

Wyn kissed the inside of her wrist. "You and me are gonna have to come up with a whole new way to communicate, Kentucky."

"Agreed."

He popped the buttons on her pearl snap shirt and tugged it off. He pulled her T-shirt over her head, glad to see she'd taken his advice to dress in layers. He unhooked her bra. He forced himself not to focus on how quickly her nipples puckered into tight points.

"Are you stripping me down completely?"

"Yeah."

"What if I get cold?"

"I'll keep you warm. Stand." He dropped to his knees and undid her belt, then her jeans. He peeled the denim down her thighs and held onto her arm as she kicked them aside. He pressed a soft kiss to her belly as he pulled off her panties. Then he wrapped his arms around her, breathed her in and released all the tension he'd carried in the past hour and a half. She was all right. Soft and warm and in his room, with him, where she belonged.

"Wynton."

"Give me a sec."

Melissa sifted her fingers through his hair. "I'm okay."

"You scared me."

"I scared myself." She clamped her hands around his jaw and tilted his head back. "I'm sorry I scared you. And we'll talk about everything after I've had some time to recover. But for right now, can I please get under the covers? I'm freezing my ass off."

He smiled against her stomach.

When he reached down to remove her socks and she said, "Huh-uh, cowboy. I'll let you strip me naked, but one of the fun side effects of diabetes is my feet are always cold, so the socks stay on."

"Yes, ma'am." Wyn rolled back the bedding. Then he stood and shed his clothes.

From beneath the covers, Melissa stared at his crotch and said, "You're hard."

"Seein' you naked does that to me. It'll behave, I promise."

"You sound like *it* has a mind of its own."

Wyn slipped in next to her. "Sometimes, I swear it does." He tucked her head under his chin and wrapped her in his arms. A sense of peace settled over him as he drifted off.

"Wynton?" she murmured.

"Yeah, baby?"

"I never want to sleep away from you again."

He kissed the top of her head. "Same here."

Chapter Ten

When Mel woke up, she had that same panicked sense of disorientation as she did when she came to on the couch in the living room.

"It's okay. You're still in my bed."

She shifted toward his voice and noticed he was propped up against the headboard, a laptop open on top of a pillow. "Surfing porn sites while I sleep, Super Man-Slut?"

He grinned. "Dammit. Why didn't I think of usin' the Internet to find porn sites? I'm usin' it for pesky research."

Her chest tightened. "What kind of research?"

"Small engine repair for this motor I plan to rebuild."

"Really?"

Wynton rolled his eyes. "No, not really. I'm finding out everything I need to know about type 1 diabetes. You got a problem with that?"

"No." She flopped back into the pillows. "I'd tell you that you could ask me anything you wanted to know, but that's sort of the whole point, isn't it? I *didn't* do that."

"Yeah." He set her blood glucose meter on her chest. "And so the fun begins. It's been two hours, so time to check those levels again."

Her eyes narrowed. "You want to watch?"

"I need to watch so I know how to do it if I ever have to. I also want to watch so I know what you deal with every day. How it's part of your routine."

Stupid, sweet man. Now he was gonna make her cry. "I need the box of glucose test strips, the box of lancets, and the alcohol swabs." She went through the process, poking herself, putting the drop of blood on the glucose test strip, putting the strip in the meter and showing him where the results appeared and explaining what the number meant.

"Wait, I know what that number means. You're still on the low end, so you need to eat or drink something to boost your count and then retest in fifteen minutes."

"Wow. You are a quick study."

Wynton stroked her cheek. "I am when it matters to me."

He definitely was testing her tear threshold.

"Do you want juice? Or raisins? Or honey? Or regular soda? Or a glucose tablet?"

"Juice would be great."

He leaned over and kissed her forehead before he popped out of bed. "Don't move. I'll be right back." The man hustled out and he didn't bother to put on pants.

She loved that about him.

She loved *everything* about him.

An odd sense of…déjà vu niggled in the back of her mind.

Tell him I love him.

The few times she'd gotten to the point she had today, she'd heard from others she'd been spectacularly nasty. She'd also heard of instances where a person blurted out secrets with no recollection of it. So had she confessed her feelings for him? To him?

Given how unbelievably close they'd gotten in the last three weeks, it wasn't a surprise that she'd fallen head over heels in love with Wynton Grant. The man was beyond amazing. But she hadn't wanted him to find out that way, when she wasn't even aware of what she was saying.

But on the other hand, it would be weird if she asked him if she'd confessed her love for him. *Hey, sexy rancher man, I'm not sure if you caught it before because I'm not even sure that I said it, but I love the fuck out of you.*

Ugh. No. That would *not* be cool.

Wynton returned with a tray. He set it on the dresser and handed her a glass of juice.

"Thank you."

"You're welcome. I'll just…" He blew out a breath. "I don't know what the fuck to do. I have so damned many questions but I don't want to bombard you."

Mel sipped the cranberry juice. "Bombard away."

"How long have you had diabetes?"

"Six and a half months."

That surprised him.

"Yeah, it's a new thing to me too. Several months before I was diagnosed I had all the classic symptoms—excessive thirst, weight loss, irritability, no appetite. I chalked it up to the end of the season stress. Then I blacked out, much like I did here today. It scared me and I went to the ER. They ran tests. The results surprised the medical staff as much as it did me because at my age it's almost always a diagnosis of type 2 diabetes, not type 1. So I spent two weeks learning that burying my head in the sand and pretending it would go away isn't the best way to deal with it."

"What happened before?"

She took another swig of juice. "I was lethargic but I competed anyway. I did great in the first go. I did fine in the team penning round. But I was the next to last competitor of the day in the cutting competition and I almost passed out. Hearing people describe the run, they said I sat atop Plato as if I'd been hypnotized."

Wynton brushed her hair out of her face. "Is that how you remembered it?"

"That's the thing. I *don't* remember anything at all. Not dealing with my horse or even getting back to my horse trailer. I woke up the next morning and it was a worse feeling than a blackout drunk."

He kissed her forehead. "Keep goin'."

"That's when I went to the ER. After my diabetes crash course, I took Plato back to Gradsky's because I knew I had to give up competing. I blurted out everything to Berlin. She swore she'd keep it between us. But she insisted I stick around there until I got a better handle on how to live with diabetes and what was next in my life. I avoided everyone in the world of rodeo. I even avoided London when she came home."

"So that's what Breck meant when he said you were—"

"All plumped up again? Yes. I'd lost thirty pounds over the course of three months, so I probably did look anorexic."

"Still makes him a fuckin' ass for sayin' that shit to you." He absentmindedly stroked her arm. "So you've been hiding?"

"Pretty much."

"You don't gotta hide from me."

Please don't ask me right now why I didn't tell you. Because you're not running scared after finding out makes me hope this isn't the end. She pointed to the tray. "Could I get some beef jerky and one of those hard candies?"

"You bet."

"You really did do your homework."

"Like I said, I pay attention when it matters." Wynton pinned her with a look. "And in case that ain't plain enough for you, I'll repeat it. You matter to me, Melissa Lockhart. A whole heckuva lot."

She burst into tears.

Wynton thought he'd said the wrong thing, and Mel tried to get him to quit backtracking, at least until she got control of her emotions.

But the man didn't let her sob into her pillow. He simply picked her up and hauled her onto his lap, forcing her tears to fall on his chest. He murmured unintelligible things, but they soothed her with their intent.

After she settled, Wynton kissed the tears from her face. "It wrecks me to see you cryin'. Guts me like nothin' else. Except seein' you unresponsive in the barn." He rested his forehead to hers. "I still have a ton of questions, but I'll let it be for now. You test your level and then rest a little longer."

"Will you stay in here with me?"

"If you want."

"I do."

He grinned. "See? That wasn't so hard, was it?"

Chapter Eleven

Wyn had thrown a roast, potatoes, and veggies in the slow cooker before they'd loaded cattle earlier this morning, so at least he could feed her properly.

While she'd slept he'd texted Cres, letting him know she was doing better.

He'd done a little more research online.

But the answer he needed the most he could only get from her.

Melissa wandered into the kitchen. "Hey. You let me sleep a long time."

"You needed it." He kicked out a stool. "Have a seat. We can eat whenever you're ready."

"Smells good. What is it?"

"Roast. My mom's recipe. I followed it to the letter so I didn't screw it up. I'm not so good at improvising."

She gave him a smug look. "Maybe not when it comes to cooking."

"True. Is there anything you need to do before we eat?"

"No. I'll shower after dinner. Is there anything I can help you with?"

Wyn shook his head. "It's a one pot deal so I'll just plop it on the counter and dish it up."

Although they sat side by side, they didn't talk during the meal. He kept sneaking looks at her to see if she was really enjoying the food or if she was just pushing it around on her plate. But her plate was nearly empty.

"Stop looking at me out of the corner of your eye. I'm fine."

He faced her. "It's not that."

"Then what?"

"I'm embarrassed that this is the first time I've cooked for you in my home. I never thought I'd be the type of guy who'd take for granted that you'd cook for me when you stayed here because you're a woman."

She set her hand on his arm. "I cooked for us because I like to cook. And since you've been stewing about this you probably know that the other reason I did it was because I have dietary restrictions."

"So you wouldn't set off my warning bells if I made something that you couldn't eat. And then I wouldn't ask questions if you were doin' all the cooking."

Melissa shoved her plate across the counter. She wiped her mouth and turned her barstool toward him. "We're having this out now? Fine. Ask me."

"Why didn't you tell me?"

"Because you were supposed to be a one-night wedding hookup, Wynton."

He counted to ten. "But it didn't turn out that way. You've been livin' in my house, we've been workin' together, sorting cattle almost every day for three weeks, we've been fucking like bunnies…and not once when you were scurrying off to your room to test your blood sugar and inject yourself with insulin did it ever occur to you to tell me that you're diabetic? And that you could have some sort of serious episode that might send you into a coma? I keep thinking how goddamned glad I am that Mick came back here and had the experience to know all wasn't right with you. Do you have any idea how it made me feel that I didn't know my lover has a life-threatening disease? That I wouldn't know what the fuck to do if something like that happened when we were alone? That you could've died because I wouldn't have known how to help you? That flat out sucks, Melissa. And I know this ain't about me, but goddammit, you *know* it was wrong to keep this from me for even a day, let alone fuckin' weeks!"

Wyn's voice had escalated and he shrank back away from her. Shit. He hadn't meant to yell at her. He scrubbed his hands over his face. "Fuck. Sorry. I just…" He pushed back from the counter.

"Wynton—"

He held up his hand. "Just give me a minute." He walked to the back door. The day had stayed warm and although the sun had set, he welcomed the breeze blowing through the screen, needing something to cool him off because he hadn't gotten a handle on his temper like he thought he had.

Soft arms circled his waist. Melissa rested her cheek on his shoulder blade. "I'm sorry. I can't say that enough and mean it enough. I never wanted you to see me like that."

"Which is why you didn't tell me?"

Her sigh warmed his shirt where her mouth rested. "No. I didn't tell you because I worried that it'd spook you."

"Why in the hell would you think that?"

"Um, I was at the hospital with you during your dad's ordeal, remember? And we had a few conversations about how you didn't know how to deal with health crises situations. You said you either shut down or used avoidance. You admitted you were freaked out by Sutton's injuries—both times—and how relieved you were that he made a full recovery because you weren't sure you could handle him being permanently damaged. So tell me, I was just supposed to blurt out that I have a condition that might end up blinding me? Making me lose a limb? That I had to deal with medication and monitoring every day for the rest of my life? You would've said, 'Thanks for telling me, Melissa. I know we haven't even been on one date yet, but I want to learn everything about your condition on the off chance that I'm not freaked out by helping you deal with this every day forever.' That's bullshit and you know it."

She was right. Fuck he *hated* that she was right. She hadn't even mentioned how horrified he'd been that she had dealt with a permanently injured sibling. And she hadn't called him out on his less than grateful attitude that he'd been spared that.

"Do you want to know how my mother reacted when I told her? She tried to convince me that I was mistaken. I couldn't possibly have 'contracted' type 1 diabetes as a thirty-two-year-old woman. She got all haughty and informed me that what I meant was I had type 2 diabetes. And well, she had little sympathy for me because everyone knows that type 2 diabetes is a disease fat, lazy people and alcoholics bring on themselves by not taking care of themselves."

Wyn didn't know if he could stomach any more of this.

You will listen, asshole. You're the one who demanded to know why she hadn't told you. Now that she has the guts to do so, you ain't gonna puss out.

"Then she said she couldn't believe I was making such a big deal about it. That there were people like Alyssa with real physical problems that couldn't be fixed by a change in diet and exercise. And it was sad that I needed attention for a situation of my own making, and I should be ashamed. That I shouldn't contact them again until I got my life in order."

He spun around and gathered her into his arms when the sobs broke free. "Baby, I'm so sorry."

"So you can see why I'd be less than eager to relive *that* experience."

"No offense, but your family is a bunch of fucking idiots."

"It still hurts."

"I can't imagine." He kissed the top of her head. "Did your sister react the same way?"

"I haven't told her."

"I'm sensing a pattern here, Kentucky."

Melissa head-butted his chest. "I'm sorry I didn't tell you. I haven't told Alyssa because she's been in Europe for fucking ever and I haven't talked to her." She looked at him. "Are you ever going to forgive me for not telling you?"

"Yes. If you'll let us start over."

"Meaning what?"

He took the biggest chance of his life. "As much as I'd like to pretend this has only been about sex between us, that's a lie. It's been about more than that since the second you walked into the hospital and stayed with me all night. I like being around you. I like having you in my house and part of my life."

"I-I don't know what to say."

"Say you'll give me a chance—us a chance."

"I'm supposed to leave tomorrow."

Wyn kissed her. "I know. I'm askin' you to rethink that."

Those soulful brown eyes searched his. "What happened today hasn't scared you off?"

"Exactly the opposite." *It makes me want to hold on to you tighter. It makes me want to prove to you that I can love you like no one else can. It makes me think I've been single all these years because I was waiting for you.*

She sighed and snuggled into him. "You make my head spin, Wynton Grant."

"Is that a good thing?"

"A very good thing. Now, can we curl up on the couch and watch *South Park*?"

"Yeah. Hearing you laugh will do me a world of good, Kentucky."

"I was thinking the same thing about you, cowboy."

* * * *

When Mel felt so restless she thought she might crawl out of her skin, she told him she needed an orgasm to relax.

He told her to take a shower. And he insisted she clean up in his master bathroom since his huge shower had a bench seat in case she got tired.

The man was still babying her.

She sort of loved it.

As hard as she tried to convince him he didn't have to sit on the vanity and watch her, the stubborn man didn't listen.

After she'd washed and conditioned her hair, shaved and loofah-ed her skin with her favorite lavender vanilla body wash, she rinsed off and decided to put her plan to get a little action into action. But the man usurped her intent to give him a show—rubbing one out while sitting on the bench, her legs spread wide—when he entered the shower completely naked with that wicked gleam in his eyes.

"I could tell by the way your ass twitched that you were up to no good, Amazing Slut-Girl. So if you're feelin' up to teasing me then I figure you're up for this." He dropped to his knees and pulled her to the edge of the bench. "Brace yourself, arms behind you." Then he nuzzled her patch of pubic hair and slid his tongue up and down her slit.

"You are so very, very good at that, Super Man-Slut." Melissa felt dizzy for an entirely different reason, but she wouldn't tell him because he might stop doing that swirling thing with his tongue.

Wynton wasn't in a teasing mood. He ate at her as if he was starved for her. The water from the shower flowed over her skin like a dozen softly caressing fingers. Tiny sparkling droplets beaded on his face, the ends of his hair, and those amazingly long eyelashes. His fingers tightened on her ass and he stopped sucking to growl, "Fuck. I know where all the sugar in your body has gone to. Right here. Christ. You're as sweet and addictive as candy."

She trembled at the power behind his meaning. "Wynton. Please."

"Give it to me."

"I am."

"You're holding back. I wanna feel you explode on my tongue."

"Then stop talking and put your mouth back on my clit," she retorted.

His laughter vibrating on her swollen tissues had her gasping.

And the man knew just how to use that skilled tongue.

She shattered—the pulsing, pounding, dizzying orgasm sent her soaring to that other white void.

When she floated back down and opened her eyes, she saw something she'd never wanted to see on her lover's face. Concern.

He opened his mouth—probably to ask if she was okay—and she placed her fingers over his lips.

"Don't. I feel great. I want to feel even better. So get up here and fuck me. I want to lose myself in you for a little while." She scraped her fingers across the dark stubble on his cheeks, loving how the water had softened those bristly hairs. "There's something else I didn't tell you."

"What?"

"You're the first man I've been with since I was diagnosed."

"Why me?"

"Because you're like me—or the me I used to be before. Unapologetically sexual. I liked the way you just took over. I've never had that. Never needed it. Never wanted it. So once we got past the first couple of times we were naked together, I thought if you noticed the insulin injection sites while we were rolling around in the sheets then it wouldn't be as big a deal. That I could tell you the truth and maybe you wouldn't kick me out of bed. When you didn't notice them, for the first time in six months I felt like myself again. You have no idea what that meant to me."

"Yeah, baby, I think I do." Wynton kissed his way up her body, stopping to lick the water off her nipples. When he reached her neck, he sucked and nuzzled the spot that made her wet, made her wiggle, made her moan. "When I was in your room earlier I noticed a package of birth control pills on the dresser. You've been taking the pill?"

"Yes. Why?"

"Because I want you bare. No barriers between us. I'm clean. I haven't been with anyone in eight months." He brushed his lips over her ear. "I've never had sex without a condom."

She pushed him back to stare into his eyes. "Never?"

"Never. I've haven't been interested in a long-term relationship. Until now. Until you, Melissa."

It took every bit of control for her not to burst into tears. She managed to keep her tone light. "Lucky for you I'm so wet we won't even need lube since we won't be using a lubed up condom."

He kissed her then. Kissed her and pulled her into his arms. He maneuvered them so he was sitting on the bench and they were face to face. "You're beautiful."

"You don't have to flatter me. I'm a sure thing, Wynton."

"You're still beautiful." When he kissed her like she was precious to him, and not as if he was being careful because she was fragile, she understood his tenderness came from his strength. And she loved him all the more for it.

Locking her ankles around his lower back, she draped her forearms on his shoulders. When she felt him position the head of his cock at her entrance, she whispered, "Go slowly so I can watch your face."

Wynton kept one hand on her ass and the other cupped her neck as he eased into her fully. "Oh yeah. That feels fucking fantastic."

"Make this last. I want to feel you fill me every single time."

He groaned. "Babe. Cut me a break. The first time with no condom. I don't know how long I can last."

They moved together slowly, taking time to kiss and taste and caress.

And when he couldn't hold back any longer, she slipped her hand between their bodies and got herself off the same time he bathed her pussy in his liquid heat.

Only after he kissed her did she notice he'd turned the water off.

"Did you mean it?" he whispered.

"Mean what?"

"Mean it when you said, *tell him I love him*."

Her heart raced. "I didn't think you heard that."

"I did. And I want to know if you meant it."

"Yes, I meant it."

He smiled against her neck.

"Wynton. This is where you tell me this isn't logical. That it's crazy I fell in love with you in three weeks."

"I can't do that. I'm suffering from the same lack of logic, Kentucky, because I fell in love with you too."

Mel eased back and looked into his eyes.

"Don't go tomorrow. Stay with me."

"For how long?"

"Just until the end of time."

She laughed. But her smile faded when she realized he wasn't joking. "Are you sure? Everything is up in the air with me."

"Those things would still be up in the air regardless if you were here or in Timbuktu."

"You do have a point."

He rested his forehead to hers. "Let's figure some of this out together."

"No rush?"

"None."

"Okay."

Chapter Twelve

One week later...

Mel's phone rang and her pulse jumped, as it always did when she saw her sister's name on the caller ID. "Hello?"

"What the hell, sis? I just found out that you have type 2 diabetes?"

"Hi Alyssa, long time no talk. How are you?"

"Pissed. God. I've been gone to Europe for eight months and I don't hear from you at all—we'll get into that bullshit in a minute. So when I ask Mom how you're doing, she just casually fucking mentions that you have 'contracted' diabetes, like it's some kind of venereal disease?"

Mel laughed. She loved her sister. Over the years, Alyssa had taken total control of her life. She didn't take shit from anyone, including their parents, and she'd plow over anyone who got in her way of achieving her many goals. The woman was a muscular beast—on her upper half anyway—and she could inflict some serious damage on anyone dumb enough to assume that being paralyzed from the waist down meant that her brain was somehow impaired. "I can say this to you because you understand, but Mom was a stone-cold bitch when I told her about my diagnosis. And I don't have type 2 diabetes, I have type 1. Which means I'll be insulin dependent for the rest of my life. Of course, Mom being the medical expert on all things insisted I didn't know my own diagnosis."

"Are you kidding me?"

"Nope." And because it felt good to get all of this off her chest with Wynton, she did it again, detailing the entire conversation between her and their mother.

Alyssa was so quiet for so long afterward that Mel thought they'd gotten disconnected.

"Hello?"

"I'm still here. Checking my blood pressure because I'm fuming so hard. First of all, it sucks that not only did you discover you have a serious health issue, you didn't have family support after you found out." She paused. "You didn't keep me out of the loop about your diagnosis to pay me back for bein' such a sorry-assed cunt to you after my accident?"

Mel snorted. How had she forgotten that bloody cunt and sorry-assed cunt were her sister's favorite words? "God, no. I knew you were rolling across the globe, being the world spokeswoman for impaired athletes and inspiring millions. I didn't want to burden you."

"Burden me," Alyssa repeated. "That's horseshit. You've supported me through more than I care to think about. You should've let me rot in my own misery, but you didn't. And it sucks that you wouldn't allow me to be there for you. You didn't have the right to take that away from me. Yeah, I probably wouldn't have flown home, but goddammit, Mel, I have a fucking phone. We could've talked about it."

"I never knew what time zone you were in and international calls are expensive."

Alyssa snarled, "Expensive? What the ever-loving fuck? Jesus, Mel, we both have a damn trust fund! Money hasn't ever been an issue, nor will it ever be. Try again."

Wynton strolled into the kitchen and smiled at her. But his smile dried when he saw she was on the phone. He mouthed, "You okay?"

She nodded.

"Still waiting *Mel-is-sa*." Alyssa singsonged her full name like their mother used to.

"After I told you how Mom reacted, you're honestly surprised that I didn't break my finger trying to dial you up to sob on your shoulder?"

"Fine. You've got me there. But the fact is, I'm back in the States now. I missed you. I want to catch up on your wild, on-the-road rodeo tales. Isn't it about time for national championships to start?"

"Yeah, but I sorta…gave up competing after my diagnosis."

Silence. "Gave up. Please don't tell me it's some kind of stupid safety rule the organization enforces and you're being discriminated against due to your health impairment. Because you know I have a team of lawyers who love to go after those kinds of cases."

"Simmer down, crusader. I had a couple of episodes where I put myself, my horse, and the others in the corral with me in danger. It spooked me. So I've been taking stock."

"That better not be Mel-speak for quitting."

"And if it is?"

"I'll harass you endlessly. And you have to listen to me because I'm *paralyzed* and I still compete."

"Omigod, Alyssa. You do *not* get to play the paralyzed card with me!" She shot Wynton a look and he seemed...shocked by the conversation. Most people would be, but this is how it was between her and her sister, and she wouldn't have it any other way.

Alyssa laughed. "Wrong. I *always* get to play the paralyzed card." She paused. "The question is...do you miss competing?"

Mel locked gazes with Wynton. "Actually, no. I don't miss it as much as I thought I would. I'm thinking about getting my teaching certificate so I can torture teens with words instead of a riding crop."

"You'd kill at that, sis. Good for you."

"Oh, and I *am* utilizing all the equestrian skills I've learned over the years. I've been helping out at this beautiful ranch in Colorado. I've even got this smokin' hot cowboy rancher who wants me to stick around and be his personal ranch hand. He's the lucky one I've been showing all my best riding tricks."

Wynton grinned.

"You have a boyfriend! Is it serious?"

"Yes, it's serious."

"I want to meet this guy," Alyssa demanded.

To Wynton, Mel said, "Alyssa is demanding to meet you."

"She's welcome here any time. I'll even install a wheelchair ramp for her."

She melted. She mouthed, "I love you," at him before she said, "Did you hear that?" to her sister.

"Yes, I heard that and I think I'm a little bit in love with him. Does he have a brother?"

"He has two brothers, but one is married and the other one is gay."

"Story of my life. I'm happy for you sis. Truly."

"Thanks."

"Take care of yourself. You've been feeling okay?"

How weird to have her sister asking about *her* health. "I still miscalculate sometimes, but I'm in the beginning stage of learning to live with it."

"Call me whenever you need someone to listen."

"I will."

"Okay. Love you, and be expecting a phone call from Mom at some point this week because I am going to ream her—and Dad—a new one. It's going to be fucking epic."

Mel was still smiling when she hung up.

Then Wynton was right there, curling his hands around her face.

"Sounded like that went...well."

"Alyssa is pissed on my behalf. She can lay on the guilt trip to our folks way better than I can, so I'll let her."

"I can't wait to meet her." He paused. "You're serious about looking in to getting a teaching certificate?"

"It's something I always wanted to do, but I've been too unsettled to follow through with it. Being with you...I feel settled for the first time ever, and not because I settled. But because I'm finally where I'm meant to be."

"I couldn't agree more." He kissed her and chuckled against her mouth.

"What's so funny?"

"Remember one of the first nights you stayed here and we were talking about the difference between love and lust? I told you I warned Sutton that no one falls in love in a month? And you admitted you told London the same thing?"

"Yes. Why?"

"Because we beat them by falling in love in three weeks."

Mel sighed. "Is everything always going to be a competition between you and your brothers?"

"Probably."

"You know, London and Sutton are going to take full credit for us getting together."

"Let 'em. You and I will always know the truth."

"Which is?"

"Super Man-Slut and the Amazing Slut-Girl were destined to hook up and then hang up their unopened packets of condoms for good so they could become the one and only for each other, forever."

"I love a happy ending."

"Me too." He scooped her into his arms. "Speaking of happy endings...you owe me one, woman."

"Hey, I thought you owed *me* one."

Wynton gave her a depraved look that sent her pulse tripping. "You thinking what I'm thinking?"

"Uh-huh."

Then they said *sixty-nine* simultaneously.

And they both got their happy ending...

Sign up for the 1001 Dark Nights Newsletter
and be entered to win a Tiffany Key necklace.

There's a contest every month!

Go to www.1001DarkNights.com to subscribe.

As a bonus, all subscribers will receive a free
1001 Dark Nights story
The First Night
by Lexi Blake & M.J. Rose

Turn the page for a full list of the
1001 Dark Nights fabulous novellas...

1001 Dark Nights

WICKED WOLF by Carrie Ann Ryan
A Redwood Pack Novella

WHEN IRISH EYES ARE HAUNTING by Heather Graham
A Krewe of Hunters Novella

EASY WITH YOU by Kristen Proby
A With Me In Seattle Novella

MASTER OF FREEDOM by Cherise Sinclair
A Mountain Masters Novella

CARESS OF PLEASURE by Julie Kenner
A Dark Pleasures Novella

ADORED by Lexi Blake
A Masters and Mercenaries Novella

HADES by Larissa Ione
A Demonica Novella

RAVAGED by Elisabeth Naughton
An Eternal Guardians Novella

DREAM OF YOU by Jennifer L. Armentrout
A Wait For You Novella

STRIPPED DOWN by Lorelei James
A Blacktop Cowboys ® Novella

RAGE/KILLIAN by Alexandra Ivy/Laura Wright
Bayou Heat Novellas

DRAGON KING by Donna Grant
A Dark Kings Novella

PURE WICKED by Shayla Black
A Wicked Lovers Novella

HARD AS STEEL by Laura Kaye
A Hard Ink/Raven Riders Crossover

STROKE OF MIDNIGHT by Lara Adrian
A Midnight Breed Novella

ALL HALLOWS EVE by Heather Graham
A Krewe of Hunters Novella

KISS THE FLAME by Christopher Rice
A Desire Exchange Novella

DARING HER LOVE by Melissa Foster
A Bradens Novella

TEASED by Rebecca Zanetti
A Dark Protectors Novella

THE PROMISE OF SURRENDER by Liliana Hart
A MacKenzie Family Novella

FOREVER WICKED by Shayla Black
A Wicked Lovers Novella

CRIMSON TWILIGHT by Heather Graham
A Krewe of Hunters Novella

CAPTURED IN SURRENDER by Liliana Hart
A MacKenzie Family Novella

SILENT BITE: A SCANGUARDS WEDDING by Tina Folsom
A Scanguards Vampire Novella

DUNGEON GAMES by Lexi Blake
A Masters and Mercenaries Novella

AZAGOTH by Larissa Ione
A Demonica Novella

NEED YOU NOW by Lisa Renee Jones
A Shattered Promises Series Prelude

SHOW ME, BABY by Cherise Sinclair
A Masters of the Shadowlands Novella

ROPED IN by Lorelei James
A Blacktop Cowboys ® Novella

TEMPTED BY MIDNIGHT by Lara Adrian
A Midnight Breed Novella

THE FLAME by Christopher Rice
A Desire Exchange Novella

CARESS OF DARKNESS by Julie Kenner
A Dark Pleasures Novella

Also from Evil Eye Concepts:

TAME ME by J. Kenner
A Stark International Novella

THE SURRENDER GATE By Christopher Rice
A Desire Exchange Novel

SERVICING THE TARGET By Cherise Sinclair
A Masters of the Shadowlands Novel

Bundles:
BUNDLE ONE
*Includes Forever Wicked by Shayla Black
Crimson Twilight by Heather Graham
Captured in Surrender by Liliana Hart
Silent Bite by Tina Folsom*

BUNDLE TWO
Includes Dungeon Games by Lexi Blake
Azagoth by Larissa Ione
Need You Now by Lisa Renee Jones
Show My, Baby by Cherise Sinclair

BUNDLE THREE
Includes Roped In by Lorelei James
Tempted By Midnight by Lara Adrian
The Flame by Christopher Rice
Caress of Darkness by Julie Kenner

About Lorelei James

Lorelei James is the *New York Times* and *USA Today* bestselling author of contemporary erotic romances in the Rough Riders, Blacktop Cowboys, and Mastered series. She also writes dark, gritty mysteries under the name Lori Armstrong and her books have won the Shamus Award and the Willa Cather Literary Award. She lives in western South Dakota.

Connect with Lorelei in the following places:

Website: http://www.loreleijames.com/

Facebook: https://www.facebook.com/LoreleiJamesAuthor

Twitter: http://twitter.com/loreleijames

Instagram: https://instagram.com/loreleijamesauthor/

Facebook Reader Discussion Group: https://www.facebook.com/groups/loreleijamesstreetteam/

Newsletter: http://loreleijames.com/newsletter.php

Roped In
A Blacktop Cowboys® Novella
By Lorelei James
Now Available!

Ambition has always been his biggest downfall...until he meets her.

World champion bulldogger Sutton Grant works hard on the road, but his quiet charm has earned the nickname "The Saint" because he's never been the love 'em and leave 'em type with the ladies. When he's sidelined by an injury, he needs help keeping his horse in competition shape, but he fears trying to sweet-talk premier horse trainer London Gradsky is a losing proposition--because the woman sorta despises him.

London is humiliated when her boyfriend dumps her for a rodeo queen. What makes the situation worse? She's forced to see the lovebirds on the rodeo circuit every weekend. In an attempt to save face, London agrees to assist the notoriously mild, but ruggedly handsome Sutton Grant with his horse training problem on one condition: Sutton has to pretend to be her new boyfriend.

But make believe doesn't last long between the sassy cowgirl and the laid-back bulldogger. When the attraction between them ignites, London learns that sexy Sutton is no Saint when that bedroom door closes; he's the red-hot lover she's always dreamed of.

The more time they spend together, the more Sutton realizes he wouldn't mind being roped and tied to the rough and tumble cowgirl for real...

* * * *

"Why me?"

"Because we both know the only people who've been able to work with him have been you and me."

She sucked in a few breaths and forced herself to loosen her fists. "This wouldn't be an issue if you hadn't browbeaten my folks into selling Dial to you outright. When the breeder owns the horse and a rider goes down, other people are in place to keep the horse conditioned. That responsibility isn't pushed aside."

"You think I don't know that? You think I'm feelin' good about any of this? Fuck. I hired people to work with him and the stubborn bastard chased them all off. A couple of them literally."

London smirked. "That's my boy."

"Your boy is getting fatter and meaner by the day," Sutton retorted. "I'm afraid if I let him go too much longer it'll be too late and he'll be as worthless as me."

Worthless? Dude. Look in the mirror much? How could Sutton be out of commission and still look like he'd stepped off the pages of *Buff and Beautiful Bulldogger* magazine?

"I hope the reason you're so quiet is because you're considering my offer."

London's gaze zoomed to his. "How do you know you can afford me?"

"I don't. I get that you're an expert on this particular horse and I'm willing to pay you for that expertise." Sutton sidestepped her and rested his big body next to hers—close to hers—against the fence. "I know it'll sound stupid, but every time I grab the tack and head out to catch Dial to try and work him, even when I'm not supposed to, I feel his frustration that I'm not doin' more. I ain't the kind of man that sees a horse—my horse—as just a tool. Your folks knew that about me or they wouldn't have sold him to me for any amount of money."

"Yeah. I do know that," she grudgingly admitted, "but you should also know that I wouldn't be doin' this for you or the money, I'd be doin' it for Dial."

"That works for me. There's another reason that I want you. Only you."

"Which is?"

His unwavering stare unnerved her, as if he was gauging whether he could trust her. Finally he said, "Strictly between us?"

She nodded.

"If it's decided I'll never compete again, you're in the horse world more than I am and you'll ensure Dial gets where he needs to be."

London hadn't been expecting that. Sutton had paid a shit ton for Dial, and he hadn't suggested she'd help him sell the horse to a proper owner, just that she'd help him find one. In her mind that meant he really had Dial's best interest at heart. Not that she believed for an instant Sutton Grant intended to retire from steer wrestling. First off, he was barely thirty. Second, rumor had it his drive to win was as wide and deep as the Colorado River.

As she contemplated how to respond, she saw her ex, Stitch, with Princess Paige plastered to his side, meandering their direction.

Dammit. Not now.

After the incident this morning, she'd steered clear of the exhibitor's hall where the pair had handed out autographs and barf bags. She felt the overwhelming need to escape, but if she booked it across the corral, it'd look like she was running from them.

Screw that. Screw them. She was not in the wrong.

"London? You look ready to commit murder. What'd I say?"

She gazed up at him. The man was too damn good-looking, so normally she wouldn't have a shot at a man like him. But he did say he'd do *anything*...

"Okay, here's the deal. I'll work with Dial, but you've gotta do something for me. Uh, two things actually."

"Name them."

How much to tell him? She didn't want to come off desperate. Still, she opted for the truth. "Backstory: my boyfriend dumped me via text last month because he'd hooked up with a rodeo queen. Because he and I were together when I made my summer schedule, that means I will see them every fucking weekend. All summer."

"And?"

"And I don't wanna be known as that poor pathetic London Gradsky pining over her lost love."

Sutton's eyes turned shrewd. "*Are* you pining for him?"

"Mostly I'm just pissed. It needs to look like I've moved on. So I realize your nickname is 'The Saint' and you don't—"

"Don't call me that," he said crossly. "Tell me what you need."

"The first thing I'd need is you to play the part of my new boyfriend."

That shocked him, but he rallied with, "I can do that. When does this start?"

"Right now, 'cause here they come." London plastered her front to his broad chest and wreathed her arms around his neck. "And make this look like the real deal, bulldogger."

"Any part of you that's hands off for me?"

She fought the urge to roll her eyes. Of course "The Saint" would ask first. "Nope."

Sutton bestowed that fuck-me-now grin. "I can work with that." He curled one hand around the back of her neck and the other around her hip.

When it appeared he intended to take his own sweet time kissing her, she took charge, teetering on tiptoe since the man was like seven feet tall.

After the first touch of their lips, he didn't dive into her mouth in a fake show of passion. He rubbed his half-parted lips across hers, each pass silently coaxing her to open up a little more. Each tease of his breath on her damp lips made them tingle.

She muttered, "Kiss me like you mean business."

Those deceptively gentle kisses vanished and Sutton unleashed himself on her. Lust, passion, need. The kiss was way more powerful and take charge than she'd expected from a man nicknamed "The Saint."

Her mind shut down to everything but the sensuous feel of his tongue twining around hers as he explored her mouth, the soft stroking of his thumb on her cheek, and the possessive way his hand stroked her, as if it knew her intimately.

Then Sutton eased back, treating her lips to nibbles, licks, and lingering smooches. "Think they're gone?" he murmured.

"Who?"

He chuckled. "Your ex."

"Oh. Right. Them." She untwined her fingers from his soft hair and let her arms drop—slowly letting her hands flow over his neck and linebacker shoulders and that oh-so-amazing chest.

Their gazes collided the second she realized Sutton's heart beat just as crazily as hers did.

"So did that pass as the real deal kiss you wanted? Or do I need to do it again?"

Yes, please.

Don't be a pushover. Let him know who's in charge.

London smoothed her hand down her blouse. "For future reference, that type of kiss will work fine."

Sutton smirked. "It worked *fine* for me too, darlin'."

On behalf of 1001 Dark Nights,
Liz Berry and M.J. Rose would like to thank ~

Steve Berry
Doug Scofield
Kim Guidroz
Jillian Stein
InkSlinger PR
Dan Slater
Asha Hossain
Chris Graham
Pamela Jamison
Jessica Johns
Dylan Stockton
Richard Blake
BookTrib After Dark
The Dinner Party Show
and Simon Lipskar

Made in the USA
Charleston, SC
17 January 2016